STARDUST

STARDUST

A Novel

Wallace B. Rendell

iUniverse, Inc.

New York Lincoln Shanghai

STARDUST

iUniverse books may be ordered through booksellers or by contacting:

iUniverse
2021 Pine Lake Road, Suite 100
Lincoln, NE 68512
www.iuniverse.com
1-800-Authors (1-800-288-4677)

Because of the dynamic nature of the Internet, any Web addresses
or links contained in this book may have changed
since publication and may no longer be valid.

This is a work of fiction. All of the characters, names, incidents, organizations,
and dialogue in this novel are either the products of the author's imagination
or are used fictitiously.

ISBN: 978-0-595-46049-6 (pbk)
ISBN: 978-0-595-70250-3 (cloth)
ISBN: 978-0-595-90349-8 (ebk)

Printed in the United States of America

To Shirley

the Group of Seven and their loves.

Fingers of light
Remove night's gown of stars
Dawn comes with avian
Choirs

The land like tumbled quilts
Slopes to a jigsaw shore
Headlands lunge large from wrinkled seas
To touch a shining multitude of clouds
A beauty quiet beyond description's cloy …

CHAPTER 1

▼

Viewed from inland, the sea cliff rose like the head of a giant turtle, its purple contours softening the sea horizon. The sky was a pageant, with the sun god and his cloudy outriders suspended in summer blue, while baleful and foreboding, an anvil-shaped cloud preened itself darkly on the northwestern horizon. The breeze rippled green water and rose up the high cliff past puffins nesting in dimpled erosions of that grey face—it lifted the sounding gulls and swayed low grasses daring to grow from mosses at cliff's edge. Here, supine among blackberries, some boy, now and always, felt summer warmth and heard the orchestra of birds, insects and the distant soothe of waves.

A few feet back from the cliff's edge the first trees clung low, thick and wonderfully green, leaning downwind in many a tortured pose. Farther back a path, reddish in decay and veined with gnarled roots, wound through balsam and birch, past a tumble of lichen-splashed rocks, then up a rise that overlooked the first house of the outport.

The house at the end of the path stood in simple square design, except for a sloping roof in which two dormer windows hinted of former pretension. Painted a now-faded green with scaling white trim, it seemed to lean on a copper beech tree that stood near the side door, a lonely survivor transplanted from England by homesick ancestors. The front steps were well scrubbed, the curtains tidy and the back garden vigorous with turnip, cabbage and potatoes. Upstairs, in the front bedroom, the sun slanted through dappled curtains, its beams illuminating dust and pictures of English country scenes hung on floral wallpaper.

Rachel lay in bed, her dark hair a nest for a face passive with resignation and fatigue. Agnes Green fluttered about. A shortened left leg from an old hip fracture caused her to lurch to port with every second step. She was the village mid-wife who lived alone up the brook. Agnes had been present all day except for brief chats with neighbours across the back fence. Picket or rigglerod fences surrounded most houses in the outports, because village horses and goats roamed freely in the summer and would make a quick feast of one's garden. The house was unusually quiet that summer afternoon as Aunt Sadie was looking after the three and five year olds, Roseanne and Tom, over in the cove. The cat watched silently from a corner chair.

"Das it my love, das it! Push a bit. The t'ird one can make a fast passage. Have a sip."

Agnes sat knitting at the foot of the bed. She was aware of tightness in her hands and she occasionally took a deep breath. It was relaxing to gaze through the window at the outport houses that lay strewn like so many coloured dice along the outcrops and gullies of the harbour shore and peaceful it was to see the boats reflecting in still water. "Sure I'm more worked up than ever since I took dem lessons from Dr O'Brien," she thought, "guess I never knew how many t'ings could go wrong." Suddenly she was aware of an oppressive feeling in the room and darkness—the motes and the sunbeams had disappeared. The curtains stirred listlessly.

Then they heard a distant rumbling, a low and prolonged growl.

The cat jumped from the chair and was gone.

"My dear! Dat's t'under and lightnin'," said Agnes, trying to keep reassurance in her voice, "We don't need to worry, no iron around 'ere. Remember 'ow upset the old folks used to get? Dey t'ought it was the Devil rollin' pork barrels. Well it's just so dark in 'ere I t'ink I'll light the lamp."

Rachel gripped the bed with the power and pain of uterine contraction, so totally autonomous—an uncontrollable force loose in her lower body. Suddenly there was a great flash. She saw the wall pictures in a cadaveric light. There was silence for a few seconds and then a shaking crash of sound like a giant fist had descended. The noise throbbed and echoed and rolled away into silence. Agnes held Rachel's hand. Now a low crescendo sound like an approaching locomotive and the wind and rain pounced. Rachel felt adrift, uncoupled from reality. The thunder seemed to mesh in time with her pains, except that it was receding and the pains were increasing to an intensity that caused a fearful intake of breath and a stifled cry. The next pain came like a rushing tide and with Agnes guiding and encouraging, Jonathan Nigel Shipman was born.

The uterine muscle, too tired to contract, allowed blood that had supplied the infant to flood into the vaginal void and out. Death smirked from the corners of the sunset room. Agnes, busy with the baby, glanced at Rachel and was startled by her facial pallor and the shiny damp of perspiration. In a rush, she threw back the sheet and saw a red tide flowing. Agnes, with pounding heart, grabbed the flaccid abdomen with both hands. The uterus felt soft and yielding. She massaged vigorously ignoring Rachel's moans of distress. Gradually, joyfully, sprinting with death, she felt the uterus firming, hardening, as contracting muscles shut off the bleeding vessels.

Two months after Jonathan's birth Rachel sat in her garden, comfortable in the lawn chair that Sam had made. A southwest breeze carried late summer warmth through the garden where lilacs were now just a memory, irises had retreated into pods, but tiger lilies and mums were stirring in full fashion. She still tired easily and was aware of her pulses throbbing as blood raced to compensate for anaemia. The baby lay unfettered in his crib, arms and legs working joyously, his eyes and face intent.

On Rachel's lap was a dog-eared copy of Harper's Bazaar dated July 1928, over a year old. Her friend Cynthia, who lived in Heart's Content, sent her magazines once in awhile from the company library there. What a treasure it was! Pictures of fashionable men and women, scenes from Chicago and New York and all over. New buildings, cars, beautiful people dancing. Architecture. What wealth! And, an ad from a university in Florida listing all the studies a person could do. What progress. The world was at peace and had been for 11 years. The war to end all wars had left a bloody stain on the Western world, but grief was giving way to a growing optimism. Sure, the telephone was available only one day away. Memorial College had opened in St. John's. Cynthia had told her that some people in the Cable Station were making all kinds of money in the New York stock market. She looked at Jonathan still fascinated by the movement of his arms and legs. What opportunities might exist for him? They were poor, but ways could be found. She nestled in the chair. The afternoon was a symphony of iridescent light, warmth and the buzz of life. She closed her eyes and watched her chameleonic retinas change slowly from dancing, dappled red to the blue-black wonder of a night sky. Jonathan blew bubbles, and she smiled.

CHAPTER 2

▼

When Jonathan Shipman was born, I was five years old and living two bays away on a rugged indented coast confronting the Atlantic Ocean. We would not meet until ten years later. Jonathan's harbour was pretty with small coves, beaches and islands; mine was big, heart shaped, with deep water coming right up to the cliffs. I guess that is why it was chosen to be part of a great technological feat.

My name is Matthew Penwell. My first memory is of leaning forward in the bow of the family boat while my father rowed toward the beach. The sunlight glinted diamonds off tiny waves, and the sea bottom—ribbed sand coloured with pebbles and shells—came steadily upwards until we hit with a grating sound, stopped quickly and I hit my nose on the stem head. Prior to that, my brain's ten billion neurons had been organizing, sending out connecting 'wires' to neighbours, stimulated by all the electronic images coming in through my senses, but it took that bump on the nose to get my memory up and running.

In my memory, childhood was one ongoing, happy adventure in a world that awed and entertained on land and sea: A continuum of birds, fish and mammals in their seasonal cycles, insects, shellfish and worms; bare feet in summer and pond skating in winter; stories told and read by the fire; other boys, even girls, and friends that came to our house and played games and sang around the piano; the sagas of brother and sisters, mom and dad; Christmas and Bonfire night; nor'easters and the wonder of the seasons, and shards of poetry and prose that would live and sustain in memory for a lifetime.

The only blemish was school, although I grudgingly soon began to realize that benefits were accruing. The main injustice was Sunday school, which seemed a very unfair interruption of the glorious freedom of the weekend, especially so as it meant having to wash, put on clean clothes and be towed about by your sister.

So much to relate. Mothering was different in those days and fathering almost non-existent in the modern sense. Do not get me wrong—in those days, being there and providing material needs and shelter, expressed love—overt demonstrations of affection—were limited and confined to women. It did seem that we were loved more on some days than others, but the thought of being unloved never occurred to us.

Small boys instinctively knew they were running a gauntlet between mothers and the temptations of the physical environment; crossing the lines for more than a brief moment earned either the wrath of mothers, or injury from water or rocks, or both. It was a stimulating challenge at all times. Girls were a mystery to us really; they liked odd things like clothes and ribbons in their hair. You never found one who liked worms or eels. They were mostly useless in a boat—you had to keep on an even keel and not use too much sail in a breeze. They seldom liked trouting and would say things like, 'how gross!', or scream when you bit a trout's head to keep it from escaping back into the water.

"What good are they?" Clyde asked, "and what will they do when they grow up?"

"Well, they'll be mothers and have to hang around inside the house a lot," said Piercey.

But Mother Nature had a game plan and, as we found out, she played her cards well!

"Be home for lunch and don't go near the harbour," a mother would say as she pushed a wool cap down over your eyes and buttoned your jacket so you could hardly breathe. Reason insisted that on this fine spring morning you were overdressed. Out of sight and sound, off came scarf and coat, which were hidden in the goat house, and you ran for the shore. Clyde and Eric and the Piercey's had already assembled. The pack ice was in. With long sticks, we arranged the pans so that several small ones, that would not support our weight, were between two stable ice platforms. The trick was to run across the pans that would tip and sink. If you were fast and nimble, you could make it. We were utilizing Archimedes's Principle and Newtonian physics. Inevitably, of course, you fell in and had the terrible feeling of North Atlantic water running into your boots. Scrambling ashore we would build a fire to dry out, or sneak into the house and sit on the kitchen couch with feet hidden under the table until dry.

Mostly we did not do bad things. Some days in the year were made for mischief, like Halloween, when people went around in the dark and did things like take gates off the hinges, turn over outhouses, or put covers over people's chimneys. One day I remember, we squeezed through a rigglerod fence into Mr. Slaughter's garden—it was barrens really—with the best kind of blueberries. Mr. Slaughter—his mother named him Will—which didn't do a thing for his image, was known to be an ogre who would make short work of anyone caught stealing his berries. So just when our hands and mouth were filled with berries, I looked up and there was this dark figure against the light, just head and shoulders visible over the knoll. Then he let out a bellow! Well my heart, which until then I didn't know was there, gave a great thump and stopped, but that didn't keep me from bolting for the fence. Clyde and Eric were ahead of me and the rigglerods were getting revenge by narrowing the gap that Eric was trying to squeeze through. It seemed to take him about three years. Fortunately, my heart had started beating again and was doing triple time and then I was through like an arrow. Lucky for us Will Slaughter was all crippled up 'with d'arthritis,' and I guess that saved me.

My sixth birthday was just three days away. Again, the mighty island lay in the gentle grip of late spring. Saturday dawned with mist on the sea that was soon to be sacrificed to the sun god now rising over the mizzen hill. I decided to visit a pond near our house to see if there were any ducks or water lilies. The path to the pond curved over barrens that were strewn with boulders of every possible size and shape, with sheep laurel, grasses and a few stunted spruce trees filling the spaces between. The ground was of an uneven nature that would challenge an athletic goat. A warm morning breeze carrying the scent of turf and grasses touched me. My eyes anticipate the next position for flying feet. Then suddenly I stop. My ears have heard a bird song. Crouching beside a small thicket, I listen and then see a bird fly—a robin. I drop to my knees and with rapid breath and increasing excitement crawl toward the small trees. Now, pushing aside bushes, I see a small mossy hollow beside a lichen-covered outcrop of stone, and there, on the whitened branch of a long dead tree, is a small circular nest containing three eggs of a most astounding blue-green colour. Knowing I was trespassing on special ground, I drew back, looking quietly for the mother, and then turned for another long look at those beautiful eggs. This would be my secret, mine alone. Telling others would increase the danger to the nest. I would return often over the next few weeks, squirming on my stomach along the mosses beneath low balsam branches, and leave a worm on a broken piece of pottery. Then one day there were three scrawny grey necks and voracious open mouths filling the nest. Years later, I would write a poem to that Robin.

The Church was where villagers went in their best clothes and more thoughtful moods to celebrate birth, death and Anglican rituals. It was a great source of pride in community achievement and, no doubt, a solace to many. To a child it was mainly wonder at graveyards with leaning stones and inscriptions of death at sea, in war and by disease, with many an age in single digits. Wonder at the size of the building, the beauty of stained glass and altar. Wonder at the reason for the crucified man that caused adults to kneel in submission. Wonder and joy at the swelling organ notes and the comfortable sense of togetherness in the great hymns. The Rector was austere, conveying a sense of power, of hierarchy. We were small, supplicant. Something here was big and controlled our destiny. Adults agreed to let control be taken from them, to literally bow down. For what reason would these adults, normally strong, independent, and resourceful, drop on their knees in submission and swear allegiance—to what? Those were the questions in my child's mind.

"Well sure b'y 'tis God," said old Isaac, puffing on a clay pipe, as we sat on the wharf watching a schooner raise anchor. "He made you and me and everything and arranges for people to go to heaven when dey die, if d'ere good," he added. "'f not, you're punished in Hell. I'm not tellin' you nothin' new. Your mother and Sunday school teacher told you all dis b'y."

"Why do they put you in the ground when you die?"

"Well, dat's just your body, 'tis your soul dat's important and it flies off."

"It flies off?"

"Yes b'y, and don't talk like this too much or yours'll fly off in the wrong direction," Isaac chuckled.

"Reverend Facey said God could calm the waves. How can he calm waves like we had last week on the Bay?"

"Will you just shut up and watch the schooner," said Isaac, with a wave of his hand.

"What about Catholics, do they have a God?"

"Well, of course, you numbskull."

"Same as ours?"

"Der's only one."

"What's the difference then in Catholics and us?"

"Dey got a Pope and der Irish. I don't know. Oh, will you shut up?"

I thought old Isaac was most likely enjoying himself. He seemed to encourage it really—like he would wink when he came around to our pew and take my dime for the collection plate. So I went back at it.

"I know the commandments," I said.

Isaac grunted, but you could see he was thinking.

"There's one that says 'Thou shalt have none other Gods but me'. Is that right?"

"Well, of course it's right," sniffed Isaac. "Moses wrote dem down on the mountain, direct from God, I'm sure 'e got it right!"

"Well, if God tells us not to have other Gods, doesn't that mean He's not the only God?"

Isaac took several puffs, shifted his weight, and stroked his beard. I waited. His eyes were intent. He reached out his hand, "Come 'ere," he said.

"You know, you're a real pain in de 'arse."

Then he grabbed me and threw me into the harbour. After that, we called him Isaac the Baptist.

One morning I walked down to the wharf to fish for conners. Isaac was sitting on the grump wearing a cap and a jacket with the collar turned up, although I thought it was quite warm.

For the first time he asked me a question. "Tim Rockwood told me the Russians have plans to send big rockets to da moon. I figured you would know about dat 'cause you do a lot of readin' down where dey have all dese books—what do dey call it?"

"The Library."

"Lie-bury," said Isaac, "sounds like a good name for a grave yard." He slapped his thigh.

"Yes" I said, "The Russians and the Americans are planning to look for life in space—on another planet."

"D'er will be no life anywhere else, I'll guarantee you dat!"

"How so?"

"Well, God took six days to make this place and what did He get? Animals all eaten' each other, people all split into t'ousands of religions each sayin' God says dere right. Dey fight among demselves. Not only dat, dey send requests to God by da millions! Fellar told me some of dem Cat'olics down on da Southern Shore, wit' da funny accents, prays t'ree or four times a day! 'Save me cat, cure old Tom!'

Da people that cause da least trouble are da ones dat don't even believe in Him! Now, on top o' dat, people are afraid to die so dey 'ave to save souls and rise from da dead. If I was God, I'd ignore all dis whinin' and I sure wouldn't start dis t'ing over anywheres else. I bet God wishes e 'ad gone fishin' for dem six days!"

It was the longest and last speech I ever heard Isaac make. Three days later, he was dead. He got a pretty good turnout. My friends went swimming, but I tagged along behind the procession. I could still hear the horse's hooves on the dirt and the creaking wheels. He didn't get the full Fisherman's Band but, one fellow brought his bugle and when he blew, the notes took a long time to die out down the valley and the birds were quiet for a spell.

Isaac's only memorial was his pipe-ash burn on the wharf. If you looked carefully at the dark spots, you could see two eyes in a face that had a half smile. Then the wind and rain took over, and in a couple of years, if you did not know any better, you would think there was nothing there.

This thing had to be taken seriously. God decreed but seemed not to interfere with me on a day-to-day basis. The whole thing seemed unreal, like a dream. But nobody could fool so many adults. Well, maybe God had charmed the adults into thinking he was something he wasn't; in some way he'd been cast in a role that was too much for him and maybe he needed my sympathy more than my allegiance. Imagine having to control the wind and the sun coming up every morning and take care of all the people and animals even!

But when you stood with all these grownups, their voices drowning out the creaking in the church rafters in a nor'easter, it was a warm and calming fellowship indeed. Here was a great mystery with no solution in sight.

It was just the next day that I thought I had angered God and that my soul was going to fly off from my body. Four of us were out at the western headlands fishing a deep area known for cod. We caught a few tomcods. It was calm. Suddenly, a pod of whales, potheads most likely, appeared at the harbour mouth. We watched those majestic mammals come on a course that would take them about 70 yards from our wee boat. When they were abreast, with boyish bravado, we picked up clamshells, the contents of which we had been using as bait, and threw them at the whales. No sooner did the shells hit the water than the entire pod turned and headed straight for our boat. What a fright. Four boys and only I could swim. No lifejackets, of course. Terror struck! We made no sound except for Jack's, "Oh my God!" On they came, massive backs and flukes, rising and falling, 30 feet … 20 feet … we regarded a monstrous death in terrified silence. Was it a dream? At 10 feet, the leaders dived. I was scared but unable to stop myself from looking down over the gunnels. There in the clear depths just below our keel passed a dozen magnificent animals, any one of which could have sent our tiny craft flying through the air. Had they had a little joke on us? It was a subdued bunch of boys that rowed quickly back to shore, relieved to stand again on solid ground with a memory that would last a lifetime.

Outside our little outport, with its unusual combination of hunter-gatherer society spiced with a dash of capitalism, events were rushing on apace. The great economic crash of 1929 had replaced the euphoria of the twenties with the gloom and deprivation of the Great Depression. An economic nightmare struck particularly hard those humans who had gathered in urban areas, dependent on other people to supply services and food. Politicians struggled with the levers of the stilled economic engine. Ideologies, always swirling in the brains of intellectuals, sought to take over the halls of economic and political power.

In Russia Communism had subdued competition and grabbed all power for the State. Man seemed susceptible to its appeal and its seeds spread and germinated rapidly throughout the planet.

Hitler secured power by ruthless suppression and, abetted by his friend, Mussolini in Italy, was preparing to unleash a malevolent political monster, beyond anyone's wildest nightmare. The planet was revolving into a cataclysm that would make mankind reassess all his beliefs in the knowledge that something was terribly wrong. What were the causes of the downfall of man and were there any solutions? What was it about the most evolved member of biology that made individuals susceptible and willing to kill and die for so many Pied Pipers?

Our outport was most fortunate. Hunter-gatherer societies are probably the happiest, as long as demand does not exceed supply. How fortunate, really, the man who could arise in the cold dawn, rub his hands before a wood fire, boil the kettle for tea and throw some bread in a bag, before leaving his modest house. No mortgage. The villagers came around and built the houses of local trees. Having stepped out of the door, he is a free man. Whether he will succeed or fail today will depend entirely upon decisions he will make. He is very sophisticated: he smells the wind, absorbs weather signs of sea and sky. He knows the cycles of the animals that will supply security for his family. His own hands have built the boat that he loves. Also, he is away from wife and small children. He has the freedom, the daily intimacy with natural things, that most of the world works all year to obtain for two weeks. External economic events mean little. He is independent, free and resourceful. There are pluses for the women as well, though maybe not as many as the man: a free hand with the children, time to feather the nest, knowledge of fruit and berries, of cooking; communication with neighbours a few feet away, time and leisure in much more abundance than the urban frenzy of self or societal imposed obligations.

Life had not changed, in essence, since October 19, 1612, when John Guy's tiny ship, Ye Endeavour, rounded the Northwest headland and he saw a large harbour unfold before him. His diary made the first mention of Heart's Content where he had a peaceful meeting with Red Indians. Then, two hundred and fifty four years later—July 27, 1866—the mightiest ship afloat, Islamabad Kingdom Brunel's Great Eastern, cleared lighthouse point and entered Heart's Content harbour, laying, like an immense spider, a cable of seven copper wires that stretched astern all the way to Valencia in Ireland. The information highway had reached North America!

A tiny fishing outport, profound in its isolation, was projected suddenly on the world's stage. With the cable came the English and with the English came gardens and soccer, a library and tennis—even cricket! At its peak, the cable station employed 200 people and transmitted data between Europe and America for 100 years before succumbing to technical obsolescence. So hunter-gathering found a core of capitalism.

There was little social friction, at least among the children. Both groups co-operated. Each was so much enamoured with the land and sea, so fascinated by what changes each season brought, that the 'isms' floating around the planet failed to take root. Also, we knew who we were. We were English, an extension of England: the first overseas colony of the greatest empire in the history of the planet. England was a magical place. We celebrated Royal occasions, admired the pictures on biscuit tins received at Christmas. There were heroes everywhere and the more one grew and read, the more the dreams expanded. Adventurers, explorers, sailors who charted the world, scientists who invented the essence of our civilization and literature—what pleasure when one first dipped a toe into the sea of British writing. The games we played! And to top it all off, to provide the final glory, more than enough for everyone forever, Britain, the Commonwealth and Empire, now stood alone on the planet, stood unflinchingly, toe to toe with the most murderous bully of all history, in defence of western civilization. It doesn't get any better than this, and we were there.

It was a Friday evening in mid-January. Yet another nor'easter howled; flung from a low that smirked with moisture over the dark ocean. The highland barrens between Trinity and Conception Bays, so recently rich with colour and life, lay blown and buried in snow. Drifts shrank the hydro poles to a few feet and levelled gullies and swales.

We waited for the mail, coming on horse drawn sleighs across the 15-mile wasteland between Carbonear and Heart's Content. The drivers, our heroes, fought to follow a tortuous road often lost in drifts and blinding squalls. The post office was the center of outport life, especially on a Friday night when we anticipated the Star Weekly with the funny papers from far off Toronto.

People had gathered by dusk and it was now 7:30 p.m. Rumours abounded. Someone had heard from the halfway house that the horses were stuck in drifts and the drivers were shovelling them out.

"Yes b'y," said Moses Underhay, a short red-faced man who had walked all the way from Lighthouse Point and was busy beating snow off his boots with his ear cap, "Mountains, yes mountains b'ys, of snow for certain on the Barrens and I allows der stuck in da Stag's Head droke."

The post office was overflowing with adults, children and the occasional dog, with barely room to move. Laughter and chatter filled the room and faded into the darkness outside. The windows steamed with humid breath. Children ran outside into the blizzard for a few minutes, returning with rosy cheeks and covered in snow.

Reflecting the outport hierarchy, some people owned mailboxes, whose glass faces looked, importantly, from one wall. The less fortunate had to wait in line at the wicket behind which appeared the bald head of the bent postman who was well aware of his importance and missed no opportunity to demonstrate authority, especially in scolding children.

"Be quiet! Get out of here!" he would bellow. "There'll be no mail for you. Get home to your mothers."

Outside it was dark, cruel, and moonless. The wind moaned. The snow shifted in mantles of white design.

A shout. "They're coming!" People rush outside.

Listen. Lean against the wind. Was it bells? Yes. Bells!

Now a creaking and trampling of hooves.

Shouts of applause!

Into the magic circle of light galloped the horses, nostrils steaming like incense around wild, snow-encrusted eyes. Riders ran alongside, red cheeks and snowy beards, in one triumphant dash. A riot of colour and animal energy. Wonder for a small boy. The mail had arrived.

Now wait as letters flick into mailboxes and people line up at the wicket. Then trudge home to wood-warmed kitchens, some clutching mail, some disappointed. The children excited to see and read the latest adventures of Dick Tracey and Smokey Stover. Weekly we walked up snow-covered hills toward home, our arms laden with books from the library. They felt warm and comforting and would transport me from my chair near the kitchen fire to join Sir Richard Grenville off Flores, or Tom Sawyer and his friend Huckleberry Finn floating down the Mississippi.

Can I say enough about words and books? The natural joys of life in a wilderness area could suffice in themselves. Oh, but what true delight to have added the wonder of words, metaphors, ideas: to grasp the tools of thought and conjecture; to have access to the distilled contemplation of the great minds of civilization; to follow the astounding progress of science as it pushes back the frontiers of ignorance; to follow the varying light of philosophy; to avoid the pitfalls of pseudo-knowledge, to walk, run, limp towards the goal of man's amazing brain; understanding the universe, even understanding itself. There is beauty everywhere and Keats justified poetry with the words, 'Beauty is truth and truth beauty ...'

There was sadness, of course, that whittled away at our innocence. Two of my friends died. One quickly, one slowly. The concepts of disease and mortality, of the precious gift of time, began to register: the sense of wrong and loss, which is the legacy of our consciousness.

Tim played soccer with us one day, rushing about after an inflated pig's bladder on a stony field. The next day his mother said his stomach was upset. Then the following day, Thursday, they called the Doctor who arrived by horse and carriage on Saturday morning. On Sunday, the blinds were pulled in the little white house over in the cove and Tim was dead. Appendicitis ruptured, the people said. We walked behind the coffin, transfixed with the thought that Tim was inside, lifeless. Something about life was wrong. Why? What was

God's role? Where was God? The search for why receded with passing time, but would not cease.

Then there was Jennifer. My sister knew Jennifer better than I did. Her dad was a Londoner employed by the cable company. She went to Boston to visit relatives and returned with tuberculosis. TB was the scourge of our Island. The disease progressed slowly but surely. The family and friends built a summer bungalow with a veranda high on north hill overlooking the harbour. They planted an English garden that bloomed in the southern exposure. Gradually she weakened as her lungs were destroyed. She was bright and cheerful. There was a mystery about the little house for us who had never been there. My sister visited. People would bring presents and entertain. Each spring and autumn a small procession would carry Jenny up to and back from her summer place. It was a mixture of beauty and pathos. One autumn the windows were boarded up for winter and never opened again.

CHAPTER 3

▼

The old man leaned on the rigglerod fence, gazing out to sea. Ten-year-old Jonathan Shipman sat on an old wood horse nearby, rubbing his aching stomach.

"How come you can't see that sandpiper just right there but you can see Dad's boat miles out to sea?" asked Jonathan.

"Huh, 'tis me age b'y. Time's a thief and he's not particular about what he steals or when. Your dad and the b'ys should be in Twillingate by tomorrow evening with this wind," old George mused, waving his hand toward the schooner, now hull down and showing only a white sail. "Good thing they have a job in the woods."

"Why no cod this year?"

"God knows. The sea is a cook like your mother—never know what she'll serve up. Caplin didn't come. One 'ting chases another."

"Think I hear mom callin'."

George straightened slowly. His left leg was sore and swollen out over his boot top.

Jonathan loved his granddad and felt sorry that he was slowed by pain and age. He had heard many stories of George's exploits as a young man when he was captain of a sixty-ton schooner; tales of daring on the Banks and at the seal hunt. And of the tragedy when the schooner 'Susan Jane' was lost and his grandmother with her.

"Let's go eat," muttered old George, "You and I are the only males in Sloop Harbour now b'y, so we better keep our strength up to look after all these women."

"What about old Steve?"

"Why he's stroked out—spends his time tryin' to make caskets with his one good arm."

They trudged up the path, the steps, and over scuffed linoleum into the kitchen's hot breath of boiled vegetables. They ate corned beef, turnip and potatoes. Jonathan ate only a few mouthfuls.

"What's wrong with you son? Come on, eat your supper."

"Don't want it. Have a feeling down here," said Jonathan, with a hand on his stomach.

"Probably eating crab apples," Rachel said. "Go up to your room and have a rest."

Rachel walked outside. She looked over the sea, past the brooding headlines to the distant blue line of the mainland. She seemed to sag with fatigue. "It's never done," she thought. "No end to it, and now Sam's gone. There's a whole world out there and I'll never see it. Stuck here, no Doctor or Priest. It's Godforsaken, really. Beautiful, they say when they come from away. Huh!"

Darkness came. The house stood gaunt in the moonlight. The sea and the land were eternal, mocking the transience of lives unfolding within weathered walls.

Lying face down, with a pillow under his stomach, Jonathan listened to the kitchen radio through the floor grating. *"The S. S. Kyle left Springdale this morning for St. Anthony—to the Persey family in Rose B, Nancy was operated on Tuesday—doing well—To Mariah in Lady cove, eye removed Tuesday, I will be home on the fifteenth. Dr. Moore of Wesleyville will visit Shamblers Cove on Thursday and Friday."* On it went; communication between St. John's and hundreds of outports in coves, arms and inlets along 10,000 miles of seacoast.

Old George lay supine before sleep. Moonbeams softened the darkness. He could see a woman's face in the brown and white photograph on the dresser. His wife, Sophie, had perished in the wreck of the Susan Jane, a forty-ton schooner on her way to the Labrador. He had persuaded her to leave their two-year old son, Samuel, with Gramma Shipman and join him on the trip. His hands clutched the blanket as memory, vivid as reality, tortured him again: the Susan Jane was becalmed in a fog. He reckoned they were well offshore, but while listening on the bow, he heard the sound of distant surf. The darkness was assaulted by lightning followed by a low growl of thunder. Sea hands turned out and were reefing when the front hit, like a giant's fist out of the fog. He pushed Sophie into a dory lashed on deck, and was fighting with the wheel to bring the Susan Jane about, when she hit.

In his recurring nightmare, he is flying over a turmoil of ship and foam, thrown onto a ledge on the cliff. Below he sees Sophie's face in a flash of light; beautiful, white, her black hair floating like seaweed. He must save her! But in the blackness his hands will not let go of the rock. The next flash showed the face, wraithlike, floating away into greenish darkness.

The old man awakened with the dawn, his spirit heavy with the shards of dreams and terrible memories. He moved from side to side to unfasten his muscles from the night's grip. He went outside, urinated and sniffed the air. The wind was light from the southeast and there were a few mares' tails overhead. He walked to the shed, annoying the rooster, and with gnarled hands split a fir log into kindling. Soon the kettle boiled and porridge was warm on the stove.

Rachel entered into the kitchen, her residual good looks besieged by greying hair and fatigue.

"Wish I was deaf like you G'arge. You slept through the entire night I do believe. You'll miss the Second Coming if it happens during the night. I was up half the night with Jonathan. He threw up three times but seemed to settle just before dawn." Her eyes were moist and there was a quiver in the tired voice.

"Why the hell do we live in such a Godforsaken place?" She threw up her hands. "No doctor and no way of getting one." Then, in a calmer voice, "Dr. Moore will be in Shamblers Cove on Thursday. Oh well, maybe, maybe Jonathan be better when he wakes up."

George walked down to the shore, past houses with windows boarded up like bandages to soothe their abandonment. The morning was splendid with a unique illumination of sea and sky. The punt was lying in an old shed with slanted walls stained with red ochre. He had made her out of local cedar and christened her Sophie. "She'll leak like a sieve—needs to be on the bottom for a few days to plim up."

"Billy," shouts George to a boy on the beach, "Round up some more b'ys for launchin'."

Soon a gaggle of small boys runs up eager to be part of the excitement.

"Rollers in place? Heave!" George orders and the boat slides gracefully into her element. Drops of seawater pour through the dry caulking and in two hours, she has sunk to her gunnels. He climbs back up to the house, which looks rather dejected today, outlined against a sunlit fogbank rolling in from the southeast. One look at Rachel gives him the news.

"Jesus G'arge, what are we going to do? He's sick G'arge, sick. I think he's going to die if we don't do something. I've sent Linda over to widow Gordons to see if she can help with her herbs. Go see him!"

Lying on his side with his legs pulled up, Jonathan smiled weakly. George saw the terrible image of youth's perfection facing its own extinction. Eyes are sunken and a dry throat can only whisper. Jonathan's forehead is hot and his breathing rapid. George, kneeling, puts an arm around Jonathan's shoulder.

"I'll get the doctor for you b'y. He'll fix you up in no time."

The fog had settled in and the wind was fretful from the east as George prepared to leave. He would have to wait until the next morning and hope that the boat would be somewhat plimed.

Sunday dawned with a clear sky. The weak low had passed and a west wind was driving the fog offshore. The surf rolled with a moderate cadence. Jonathan had taken some fluids overnight that the widow had brought. Rachel packed bologna sandwiches, potato salad and hard tack, also tea and the black kettle. George gathered a fishing line, water and a kerosene lantern.

Village boys shouted about the beach. The boat was pulled to shore and boarded by boys with bailing cans. Gradually her gunnels rose from the water and now she rode jauntily on swells as boys scraped the last water from her bilge. Sails, oars, tiller stick, rudder, gaffs, oarlocks and food, all stored. Then the safety kit—kerosene and Seadog matches stowed in an inner tube and both ends tied with cod line.

Rachel stood on a tiny island of sea grass in the pebbled sand. Her brain was hove to in the conflicting emotions of hope for the boy and worry about the impending dangerous departure of old George. The morning light splashed strange colours on cliffs and sea and accentuated the fine wrinkles around her eyes and mouth while the wind rustled her stained apron and the flowered skirt that was hem-down on one side. George was standing at the bow of the boat; the contours of an old man etched against a bar of sunlit fog that had imposed itself between sea and sky. A chill swept through Rachel, born of the morning damp, sleeplessness and a gnawing anxiety. She walked to the water's edge and hugged old George. Their eyes met for a moment.

"How can I let you do this in that leaky old boat?" But her remonstration lacked conviction. In George's old frame resided the hope for her son's recovery—the sacrifice of the old for the young is a basic tenet of biology.

"Youth must be served," George smiled, with a dismissive wave, and lifted his swollen left leg over Sophie's gunnel. He began rowing amid shouts and waves from the shore. Gulls were all facing west on Sooley's Island. Houses, in faded pastels, moved slowly away. Water glistened in the bilge. There was a west wind outside the harbour. He shipped oars and set the sails. Alive, the little boat slid through water, which whispered beneath her transom.

As the Bay opened up, an iceberg came into view, grounded on Eagle Point, its majestic whiteness set in an emerald base. He could see the blue coast 15 miles away. There he would find the channel into the next Bay and sail another 10 miles to the doctor. After 30 minutes, water reached his feet. He bailed with one hand on the tiller. "Not a problem," he thought, "the leaking will lessen as she plims up."

Diving birds were plentiful—murrs and sea ducks. Now and then appeared the dark head of an inquisitive seal. He felt a surge of happiness—more alive than he had felt for years. Here was a chance to be useful again!

By noon, the wind had freshened and whitecaps appeared on the long swell. The little boat bounced along. He thought of reefing but decided to wait. The sea was changing now, a darker blue with hints of grey. "High comin' through' he thought. It'll likely be nor' west by late afternoon. She'll have her hands full in anything over 20 knots out here b'y."

Waves were now coming up from behind pushing her stem around. He steered carefully to avoid a broach. The foresail was wind shadowed, so, in a lull, he took it down, with flapping canvas and shaking sheets. The morning's blue coast ahead had changed to green and he could smell the wild perfume of headland turf and balsam valleys. He guessed he was one hour from the channel. The boat fairly sifted along. He was wet and chilled despite oilskins and sweaters. Bailing was frequent for she was taking water over the transom and windward side. His arms and chest were aching and there were rushes of fatigue. By 7:00 p.m., old George was the center of a boisterous scene. The dark seas had built to five or six feet across the long fetch of the Bay. "That last squall was 25 knots," he mumbled. "She's surfin'—got to hold course."

The land rushed toward him. The sun dipped below the sea horizon in a bath of vermilion, tinting summer cumulus in pinks and reds as a great cathedral of colour unfolded. Looking astern he saw a huge grey-pink moon rising over his wake—a wake that was a soft silvery plume waving towards home. A fragment of an old poem from Tennyson's *Ulysses* rushed from memory.

'The lights begin to tumble from the rocks,
The long day wanes,
The slow moon climbs,
The sea moans 'round with many voices'

His fatigue evaporated in the face of such beauty. He stood up, tearful with joy and cried out in exhilaration. The cliffs came on apace. The boat seemed suspended on a crest. Suddenly, in a surge ending in calm, he was past the channel mouth, sheltered by the western head. The boat ran on a few yards, slowing. George let go of the tiller, raising both hands in celebration. In that instant, a gust plunged down off the cliff and willy-wawed in the channel. It caught her on the lee side, the sails whipped and cracked and the boat capsized.

Sophie floated upside down, having improved buoyancy by dumping lead ballast from her bilge. Eluding the mainsail, George surfaced among a litter of oars and clothing. Gasping for breath, he held on to the hull. Frigid water penetrated his oilskins. He kicked off one rubber boot but the other clung to his swollen foot like a sea anchor. The shore was only 40 feet away. He grabbed a piece of wood and struck out. Desperation and final fatigue were taking over when his foot touched bottom and he struggled up the sand. He lay on the beach while breath returned, and mustered a thin smile of chagrin. The boat lay defeated by the sea, but she had anchored herself in one last defiant act, and gradually swung in toward him. He waded into the sea, groped a trailing main sheet, and was able to pull the punt in until Sophie grounded. Panting hard he collected the black kettle and some floating hard tack. After several failures, he managed to open the stern locker and retrieve the waterproofed lantern. Trembling with cold he pulled himself onto a mossy spot between some rocks. The matches shook in his hand. Only a few were left when the lamp wick caught fire throwing light and shadows on the gathering night. He was thankful for the lantern's warmth and light. He lay down in a hollow on dry moss, pulled branches and leaves around him and tried to sleep. Moon shadows of tortured spruce and fir strode the sand and rocks. His leg ached. The sea was a cold enchantress, taunting with the ceaseless sounds of ebb and flow. His mind an old man's attic strewn with the relics of a lifetime, a tarnished consciousness through which slithered the serpents of guilt and grief over his wife's tragic loss and the impending failure of his mission to save Jonathan. The tide rose with a swishing cadence to within a few feet of his bed. There were also currents in his internal sea: In the swollen leg, a red clot had appeared on the inner wall of an injured vein. It grew serpentine and the end of the clot weaved downstream like a fish tail in the blood streaming back to his heart.

At dawn, a boat nosed out of the channel. The bow oarsman stopped rowing to hoist a sail. A faint glimmer from the rocks caught his eye and then he saw a boat, half submerged on the shore.

✳   ✳   ✳   ✳

Nurse MacDonald met the Doctor's boat at the Government wharf. She had run the nursing station for fifteen years. Heavy set and a little bow-legged, she had an inquisitive set to her round face, as in one long accustomed to asking questions. The Doctor stepped ashore wearing oilskins and a wool cap, carrying a bag and a purposeful air.

"Morning Martha," he said in a West County accent.

"Welcome Paul. Looks like we're going to keep you busy today. I have a bite of lunch ready—your favourite speckled trout—but you'd better come to the surgery first. The Cumbys just brought in an old codger they found unconscious on Cross Island."

George lay covered with a Hudson Bay blanket. His bluish face, swollen and wrinkled like a deflating balloon, seemed strangely out of place on the white sheet.

Dr. Acton sat, chin on hand, after the examination. "Pulse 40 and irregular," he mused. "Left leg swollen, probably phlebitis. Lungs a bit congested. The immediate problem is hypothermia. Could have pneumonia or a pulmonary embolus. Let's intensify the efforts to warm him up."

Later, George was aware of light filtering into the darkness of his brain. Noticing movement, Nurse MacDonald gave him a gentle shake and he opened his eyes. An hour passed before he remembered his name. Then he became agitated and repeatedly told about Jonathan, pleading with the nurse to send the Doctor to Sloop Harbour or the boy would die. Having been reassured that the Doctor would go, George settled down and seemed composed. His vital signs were stable.

"Sit him out in the easy chair and encourage fluids," said Dr. Acton.

As George's foot touched the floor the clot in his leg broke free into the crimson tide and floated along an enlarging venous channel. Reaching the heart in seconds it slithered into the right auricle, through the tricuspid valve into the right ventricle, and then was pushed by the contracting ventricle into the pulmonary artery, where it arrested in haemodynamic chaos in the lung.

*   *   *   *

May 15. 6:45 p.m. The Barrelman. *"Now the outport messages. To Samuel Shipman at the Glendale paper mill—George passed away on Monday. Funeral tomorrow. Jonathan has ruptured appendix; going to St. John's on Northern Ranger. Rachel."*

Old Steve Blundon gave Rachel the coffin he had built for himself and set about building another with his one good arm. The Batson's old horse was rounded up and hitched to a cart on which the coffin was placed. The procession wound up the hill—women, children and a few dogs. Sally Pritchard played the coronet and they sang, '*Abide with Me*'. George was buried with his only book, a grade 7 Reader, because he liked to recite its poems.

And while stony soil rained down on the coffin of his granddad, Jonathan Shipman was on the ice flecked Atlantic, southeast of Baccalieu, lying in pain aboard the *S. S. Kyle* on his way to hospital in St. John's.

CHAPTER 4

▼

Matthew Penwell was miserable, lying in bed in the St. John's General Hospital while a late June afternoon taunted him through the dusty window. Dr. Blackler had removed his tonsils the day before. His throat hurt, his mouth was dry and he was hungry. He squirmed in a wrinkled bed and intermittently tried to read Moby Dick in the book section of an old Reader's Digest. The sound of voices and wheels on linoleum grew louder and a stretcher was wheeled into the room by an orderly in greens and an elderly nurse. A tousled boy-body was transferred to the bed next to Matt. He listened to the activity going on behind pulled curtains.

"He's almost awake," said the nurse, "I'll stay with him until the shift changes. Would you get another litre of glucose-saline?"

The curtains remained pulled all that busy night but at ten a.m. the next morning, they were opened and Matthew Penwell and Jonathan Shipman saw each other for the first time. Jonathan was weak and being fed intravenously. There was only fleeting eye contact at first, but later in the day they looked at each other with sheepish smiles, realizing that they both had been staring at a student nurse who, attempting to put Jonathan's bag on a high shelf, was exposing shapely thighs above white stockings. With that silent evidence of shared interest, a conversational bridge was built.

"What's wrong with you?" asked Jonathan.

"Tonsils out—and you?"

"Tis my appendix".

During the day, Jonathan told the story of his illness and, interrupted by sad silences, of the dramatic death of his Grandfather.

The next day they were both much improved. The conversation turned to their predicament; missing the spring unfolding of Mother Nature's treasures. They bragged about ponds, brooks and harbours of their respective outports exchanging stories of speckled trout, lobsters and the spring salmon run; the lobsters grew bigger, the eagles more numerous and the whales came closer.

In this place of white coats, strange odours and mysterious science, they longed for the freedom of land and sea. Jonathan, who had been very sick, was resigned, but when the stern Doctor told Matt he would have to stay four more days because he lived in a remote area and there was a chance of haemorrhage, his spirits sank, then rebounded, and restlessness turned to rebellion. He plotted his escape and whispered strategy with Jonathan after lights out. The next morning, with Jonathan acting as lookout, Matt retrieved his clothes, arranged a decoy patient in the bed and, with a handshake, left Jonathan and slipped out a side door into the sunlit city.

He walked through downtown streets, past jellybean houses, where lilac and laburnum were verging on bloom. He was euphoric with rebellion and anticipation. Near the Balsam Hotel, a taxi left daily for around the Bay. A few hours later, he saw familiar hills and the Harbour where the family skiff swung primly to her collar. Then he was walking up the Barren's Hill toward his house and into endless summer.

This act of defiance brought Hospital alarm and the wrath of Mother and Sisters. Moments of contrition ensued but nothing that matured into real regret.

CHAPTER 5

▼

When U694 had risen to periscope depth Cdr. Herbert Cupper scanned the sea horizon. There, bearing 278 degrees was a ship—a sailing ship! She was on the horizon but not hull-down, about seven miles away. The morning light distorted her image so that she looked levitated on the sea. He noted the long jib boom with flying jib and working jib attached, foresail and mainsail on masts whose length indicated that she was a schooner. As he watched, the vessel bore away and showed her starboard quarter. 'She's beautiful' he thought.

"Steer course 280," he ordered, "Maintain periscope depth at six knots."

The most sinister of all the terrifying weapons of war turned towards its prey.

The *Blackduck* had left the French Islands of St. Pierre and Mique-lon at dawn. She was schooner rigged, Lunenburg built and eighty-five feet in length. Several of her crew of ten men were suffer-ing from a night of carouse. Wine and women had been the attrac-tion. The wine removed their inhibitions and the pursuit of La femme exposed them to reprisals from the local males. In addition to her rather disabled crew, The *Blackduck* carried Pirate, a nine-year-old Newfoundland Dog now partially blind and slowed down by arthri-tis. He was well known and loved for miles around his home port; there were tales of his youthful exploits and his mother was famous for having saved a score of people when she swam ashore with a rope from a doomed Coaster. Pirate now spent most of his time on a pile of blankets between the port side stack of dories and the railing.

Adam Cotter sat flaking a trawl into a tub, removing seaweed and looking for tears. He was in first-year engineering and hoping for good money from the summer voyage. He was a remarkable young man, six feet two inches tall, whose size and grace of movement caught everyone's attention, and besides, he had an easygoing personality that seemed to adapt to every situation. The morning was full around him with the pleasant heave of the vessel and the rueful humour of a close-knit crew. He shot occasional glances at the sea, enjoying its summer friendly countenance. Suddenly something caught his eye—a flash of greenish white foam a few gunshots to starboard. Then, as he watched, a dark pole rose out of the sea leaving a white wake.

"Skipper!" he yelled, "Lard Jasus look! What is it?"

The deck crew watched transfixed. Crew rushed out of the fosc'le. Before their amazed and fearful eyes, a black monster emerged from the deep—the conning tower, then the deck and black hull of a submarine, water rushing and foaming around her as in protest.

"Oh my Gawd!" whispered the Skipper in an awed voice, "I hope she's one of ours!"

The submarine lay quiet for a moment, then the conning tower hatch was thrown open and armed men tumbled out and rushed down the ladder to man the gun on the foredeck.

"Huns," said the Skipper, "Shit! Malcolm, go below and hide some guns in the mast. Quick now!"

There was great activity on the sub and an inflatable flowered in the sea by her port side. A shout, staccato sounds, and bullets flew across *Blackduck*'s bow and splashed into the sea.

"Bring her into the wind and lower sails!" came in good English through a bullhorn. Now they were rowing across, the dinghy bristling with gun barrels, sometimes only helmets were visible above the swell.

The crew of the *Blackduck*, frantically furling sails, was caught in a web of fear—all except the young giant Cotter who gazed with a bemused look at the approaching threat. To the others the scene was a silent scream, a twisted pollution of their world.

As the dinghy neared, a stocky figure attempted to stand but sat quickly as the raft almost turned turtle. He had a reddish face that seemed out of place among his pale companions.

"We take command of your vessel in the name of the Third Reich," he shouted in perfect English, "Any resistance will result in death! Ladder please!" The 'please' seeming rather incongruous in the circumstances.

The submariners climbed on board. The *Blackduck's* crew were assembled amidships at gunpoint and searched. The deck was a mess of ropes and sails. A marine found Solomon Oldford, the worst casualty of the night before, sleeping in his bunk, and he was shoved at rifle point and blinking in disbelief to join the huddled crew.

The Oberlieutenant struck a victor's pose.

"This vessel will sail under German command and your captain and crew will assist or die." He looked with a swaggering distain at the ragged crew.

At that moment, Pirate padded unseen from behind the dories. He was just a few feet behind the Oberlieutenant when he let forth a huge bark. The German jumped so violently that he almost dropped his gun, his helmet slipped sideways on his head and his features froze in alarm. He whirled, levelled his revolver and fired point-blank into Pirate's head. The dog slumped in a spattering red mist and lay twitching on the deck. Solomon Oldford, with a curse, instinctively leapt to comfort his dog. The gun roared again and Solomon slumped with a dying scream and fell across old Pirate. Both bodies twisted in death and a red stream ran across the deck into the port scuppers.

Adam looked at the German's face. His colour had changed from reddish to a pale gray and his expression to one of depressed fatigue at his having shown the weakness of overreaction.

"Now you will take me seriously," he screamed.

Marines tied four of the crew to the mast in the foc'sle and the other five were ordered to get the ship underway. Two fishermen were forced to weight the bodies and throw them into the sea—dog and his master into the gray depths. With sails raised, and with a dark stain serpentine on her deck, the *Blackduck* gathered speed on a northeast course towards Cape Race.

The Submarine slipped its dark menace below the waves. For a while, a white wake followed the periscope and then suddenly the sea was without a blemish.

Each crewmember strove to control an emotional firestorm, but the horrific events they had seen on their own deck had changed the initial web of fear into a seething visceral hatred that demanded revenge.

CHAPTER 6

▼

The Shipman family had moved to Heart's Content and had now lived in the yellow house with green trim for almost a year. Rachel had insisted. The move had been no problem for Jonathan and Tom as they had the same access to the natural world and Jonathan's friendship with Matt Penwell gave them an in with the gang. Their sister Roseanne was delighted with her choice of girlfriends. Only Sam suffered the pangs of nostalgic longing for the hills and coves that were etched in the ancestral memory of his family.

The Anglo American Cable Station at Heart's Content had lain off over half the employees in the past decade. Many houses were vacant and stood gaunt in the decline of neglect; either family had moved away or the old people had died.

"Das it," said Sam "Dis 'conomy is goin' back to fishin', back to pullin' a few dollars out of the sea—if you're lucky!"

"B'y she's t'ree stories tall," Ephram commented, looking at the yellow-green house, "Tim Matthews bought old Bill's place on Rowe's Bank, t'ree stories she was too. He found 'er so 'ard to 'eat in winter that 'es knockin' the top two floors off 'er. Says 'e was 'aulin' wood from as far as Dannel's Pond and near killed 'is poor 'arse Flossie.".

"Well," said Sam, "the woman is proud, yes b'y, proud of 'er new place, so I better not start knockin' 'er down for a while, tho' I allows

I can see Tim's point. Just hope some fellar' don't show up from away and claim I'm livin' in 'is 'ouse."

Ephram was quiet for a while as though he was tired of so much talk. He walked half way across the front lawn, which was bursting with piss-a-beds and flanked by lilacs and bleeding hearts, then he stopped, spit, turned and said in a husky voice, "The Hallams down the shore just heard their son was on *HMS Hood*. T'ank God dey got the *Bismarck*." He turned and walked away.

Inside the house, Rachel sat, hands on knees, and looked at her face in the mirror. She chuckled—the caribou head mounted on the far wall was so placed that the rack seemed to be coming out of her own greying head. She had developed the habit of talking with her own mirror image. "Now," she said, "haven't you just gotten your own way all 'round; Dr. twice a week, a live-in Pastor, lot's of friendly people, running water and even a library if I can ever get time to visit. I must be happy sure, I've got everything! So why do I feel so tired and why did I burst out crying the other day when Sam tracked mud all over the kitchen? I should just have given him a wallop and made him clean up!" She looked closer at her image; greying temples, fine wrinkles around the eyes—a different look somehow—like she didn't really recognize herself. "Oh c'mon, stop imagining. Get on with it."

There were excited voices came from below and the screen door slammed.

"Mom. Mom! Just come and see. What a size of a lobster!"

Rachel smiled wanly at the caribou head as she made her way downstairs.

Tom was standing by the kitchen sink, his rubber boots decorated with seaweed and dripping salt water. He wore an expression of pure excitement and held a huge crustacean in his right hand. Matt and Jonathan crowded around in admiration.

"See, I can 'ardly lift 'im Mom! We were fishin' for conners. I was lookin' down at the white belly of a dead flatfish. Then I saw somethin' come over the white—t'was a claw! Lobster! I yelled. 'You got some eyes,' Matt said, 'he'll take bait! Let's cut up a conner!' No b'y, I says—I'm goin' to give 'im the jigger! I pulled over Mr. Sidley's boat dat was lyin' to 'er collar—I was some scared because Mr. Sidley said he'd jibbit anyone he found touching 'is boat. I dropped the jigger straight down, hit 'im on the back,—'e reared up and I hooked 'im in the claw. I could 'ardly pull 'im up!"

Roseanne had come down the stairs and stood looking at her brother with disdain. Seeing the look, Tom rushed at her with the lobster. She retreated up a few steps, and then choosing to ignore him, addressed her Mother.

"Mom, Judy asked me over to her house, she has a friend visiting from town, but I have nothing to wear! Didn't the parcel come?"

"Not yet—the catalogue said it would be six weeks. Put on your green dress."

"No! I hate it. It doesn't hang right in front!"

"It needs ironing, I expect. Go get it."

Tom, while listening to this bizarre conversation, had placed the kicking lobster in a large pot of seawater, which seemed to accentuate its astounding colours.

"Mom, when's supper?"

"You'll wait 'till I'm ready," snapped Rachel.

"Judy has a bike and she said her friend from town has a tennis racquet," said Roseanne to nobody in particular.

Rachel raised her eyebrows and stoked the fire under the potatoes.

The parcel arrived exactly five weeks after Rachel had sent the order sheet to Toronto, Canada. Roseanne was so excited she actually hugged Tom. Jonathan was also in a state of high anticipation; he was getting a new Sunday suit, and just in time as his Sunday pants were now well above his ankles. He and Mom had poured over the catalogue on a winter evening with even Sam giving advice. Page after page, how could anybody own so much stuff? Finally he picked a nice brown suit—on the bright side of brown maybe—and during the waiting weeks he often fancied himself going to Church in that new suit and the looks he would get from Suzy Cumby.

The large package was opened. Roseanne seemed to have the Lioness' share and was prancing about. Then, there it was. The Suit—a shocker!

"It's red," Jonathan complained.

"It's not red" said Rachel, "a little rust maybe, but not red!"

"Rust—rusty," said Jonathan, all enthusiasm drained from his voice. "I can't wear it! It's not the colour they showed. They'll laugh at me. Send it back!"

"Try it on," said Rachel.

Jonathan looked at himself in the mirror. He liked the fit but the colour melted his courage.

"It's great," said Rachel, "fits to a T—if I send it back to Canada, it'll take months."

"Looks grand on you," said Sam, "We'll call it your Beothuk suit."

Jonathan's mood was repressed for days. He gradually adjusted, but would forever look back on that suit as a discordant note in the harmony of his childhood.

CHAPTER 7

▼

One September morning, the sun that rose over the mizzen hill brought change. Matthew awoke to the distant staccato of a one-cylinder engine. He dressed quickly and walked outside. His mom was still asleep and dad was finishing the twelve to eight shift at the Cable Station. The fisherman's engine had died in the distance and in the silence he could hear the sounds of surf and bird song. He sat on his favourite rock on the barrens, looking at the morning light on the ponds and the Mizzen hill. The trees had matured in the late summer and the July riot of wild flowers was sleeping in seeds. A chapter was ending and a new page lay unwritten before him. He walked over and touched the smooth gray trunk of the copper beech and watched the smoking chimneys that spoke of breakfast cooking on wood stoves. His dad came into view walking slowly up the hill.

"Well, you young scallywag," said Edwin, giving Matt a one armed hug, "off to college is it? So soon it happens."

"You need some sleep Dad. Any war news overnight?"

"Lots, and not much of it good. London is being pounded from the air, I can't imagine the suffering and terror. The RAF shot down thirty seven Nazi planes yesterday—that's encouraging."

"Odds look bad now that the Russians have thrown with the Germans. Who would have dreamt that would happen."

"Bad indeed! The Empire is staggering from the loss of blood and treasure."

"I can't believe the States can stand by, making a profit, while a monster destroys Democracy."

"Well they have strong ethnic groups that hate the Brits more than the Nazis."

The conversation distracted them from the emotion of Matt's leaving.

"Right, let's have breakfast. The Brits are a resolute lot and we now have a great leader."

They had cereal and toast. Mother fussed with Matt's packing. A horn sounded; the taxi had arrived. Eyes swam with emotion.

"See you at Christmas!"

"Be true to yourself."

The car moved away along the dusty harbour road.

CHAPTER 8

▼

Matt often looked back and mused on the year that followed; a year of fun and conjecture and tragedy. There was the friendly rivalry with the townies, getting to know girls, sports, and religiosity and, of course, studies. Vast Newfoundland had only one city—St. John's, which was known everywhere as Town, and the inhabitants as Townies. Everyone else was a Bayman. The few stragglers who lived away from the coast were unclassified. The Townies had a lot of 'things' and felt superior, but he knew that the things they thought were gains were really losses and that the Bayman were inestimably more fortunate.

Matt stayed at the United Church College Residence; a large building three stories high. It was co-ed, amazingly ahead of its time, with girls on the second floor and boys on the third. The boys walked through the girl's quarters to get to their floor. This led to their being able to swivel their eyes through a greater angle than maybe any other animal.

Girls came into better focus that year; they were softer, prettier and better turned out. We were fascinated with them really and would behave strangely in their presence. There was a great interest in their anatomy. Sometimes you became so obsessed that you forgot about speckled trout fishing for days at a time. What was that all about? They were all little Mona Lisas really. They had a game plan that was much more complex than the 'one plus one having sex = mission accomplished' of the male, which, at least, had a certain mathematical integrity.

Religiosity was pronounced. The Reverend Mr. Cross was quite amiable mostly, but he set his features when he started to pray and crossed his hands on his chest so that he looked like a dead man talking. Prayers were everywhere. You could not put anything in your mouth without saying one. Sundays meant three times at Church unless you were sick, and sickness did seem more common on the Lord's Day. Then you could stay in your room and even flirt with the maids. In Church, we thanked God and beseeched him to save our King, protect our soldiers and look after us. Again the hymns saved the day; lusty singing of *'For all the Saints who from their labours rest'*, and *'Oh hear us when we cry to thee, for those in peril on the sea.'* And in peril they were. But, were the Germans not asking the same God in the same way for the same things? How could God sort this out? Mostly, wars were supposed to be fought between people who had different Gods, or at least between people who thought God was telling them different things: Then you could kill your neighbour in the name of God, which made more sense!

Sports were great. The Townies were ahead here. Around the Bay we had no coaches; our parents just fed us and sent us out the door. In Town, they had real balls and pucks! You could ride in a jeep going to the soccer game and wave at the girls! If you scored three goals you won a twelve-bottle case of coke! There was camaraderie and intense rivalry with the Catholics and even the Anglicans. It was great!

Mainly though, it was about study. There are defining moments in our lives. Matthew had entered the classroom without premonition; indeed, he was rather distracted by fatigue from a recent virus. The seat was hard, the lighting poor and this was a lecture in English Literature. The Professor walked to the lectern, black gown swishing over a gray suit. He was small. He looked at the students over his glasses and began in clear Oxford accents. "Today we will begin 'Sesame and Lilies,' of *King's Treasures*, by John Ruskin."

There followed words of such power as to be intoxicating. Mathew was elevated above the mundane as by an opiate.

"We talk of food for the mind, as of food for the body. Now a good book contains such food inexhaustibly; it is a provision for life, and for the best part of us ... meanwhile, there is a novelty continually open to us, of people who will talk to us as long as we like, whatever our rank or occupation: talk to us in the best words they can choose, and of things nearest their hearts. And this society, because it is so numerous and so gentle, can be kept waiting around us all day long, Kings and statesmen lingering patiently not to grant audience, but to gain it! In those plainly furnished and narrow anterooms, our bookcase shelves ..."

An hour later Matthew shuffled out into the sunshine with his fellow students, all more subdued than usual, like an audience that has seen great theatre. The Professor had conveyed delight in the wonder of words, the tools of thought and conjecture; the keys with which one could access the ferment of minds that worldwide were thirsting to explain the Universe, its contents, its origin. He was imbued with exhilaration for words that would endure.

CHAPTER 9

▼

Matt's parents were eating lunch. Clarissa, prim and petite, had cooked a rabbit stew—a tasty antidote to the blustery March day. Edwin Penwell looked older than his fifty years; he was bald with gray fringes over his ears and dark circles beneath deep-set eyes. His earlier athletic build had transformed to weight that slowed his movements.

"Matt should be home around nine tonight. Robert's taxi is usually on time."

"Don't like the look of that sky," Edwin commented. "The sun has a halo and looks more silver than gold—we'll likely have snow in a few hours."

"Sheila's brush," said Clarissa, with a grimace, "Is it the evening shift for you to-day?"

"Yes, but I'll get someone to spell me off so I can meet Matt."

"How are you feeling, anymore chest pains?"

"A bit tired. Dr. Rowe said he'd give me medicine if my blood pressure doesn't go down on that low salt rice diet he's going to try. Guess I'd better enjoy the rabbit while I can. He said salt cod is taking revenge on Newfoundlanders."

Later she watched him walk away down the hill to the Anglo American Cable Station. She felt wistful, with a touch of sadness, a longing for the vigour and immortality of the early years. Now the sun had set, its colours subdued by roiling cloud ramparts. The wind was fitful as darkness settled over the outport. Soon the first soft flakes fell in almost vertical array. The clock on the kitchen cupboard showed ten past ten and Clarissa had just turned from looking out at the swirling snow when she heard a sound, the door burst open and there stood Matt, a laughing veritable snowman! With a shriek, she embraced him and then grabbed the birch broom and began brushing off the snow.

"Did you see your father?"

"No, but I came up the back way. We got stuck in the snow over in southern cove—went off the road!"

At that moment, Edwin appeared out of the night. He is snowy and pale and pauses at the door, and then walks towards Matt who rushes to him.

"Matt!"

"Hello, Dad." They clasp hands; Matt puts his left arm around his dad's shoulder. He feels a shudder and sees a strange look of detachment. Edwin's eyes roll upwards, his legs collapse and he falls, contorted, to the kitchen floor. Terror! They fall, horrified, on their knees. Clarissa screams and slaps Edwin's gray face.

Matt loosens clothes helplessly amid the frightful sounds and sights of death.

"Run for the doctor!" Clarissa screams.

Again the snow, the wind, the dark path down the barren's hill, past the schoolhouse and along the road by Cumby's house. Slipping, falling, cursing, his heart pounding and soul shredding in despair. The doctor's house is dark, bleak, frozen, and lightless. He pounds on the door and screams at the window. Nothing.

Now the breathless frantic return. He sees the windows all lit. He has an urge to run away, to be lost forever in the night. The neighbours are bustling about. His dad lies dead. This bookish, gentle man, dead and covered on the kitchen floor.

The next few days are a blur of grief, returning siblings and friends bringing food. The corpse is laid out on the dining room table. The curtains are drawn. Normal things happen. Someone laughs.

His father's last touch had been Matt's hand, his last sight, Matt's face. Was there some transference, empowerment? To the weave of Matt's sadness was added a strange strand of euphoria.

CHAPTER 10

▼

The decision to study medicine had come gradually, like light on a foggy morn. He had told his father of his decision last August as they sat by a campfire in Deep Gulch; Deep Gulch where a high, contorted cliff sheltered a scimitar pebble beach from summer south-westerlies, where just offshore flatfish buried themselves in the sand and lobsters made homes among the weedy crags; this favourite place of his childhood. They had gone sailing in Siren, a shapely fourteen-foot punt. The summer wind had piped up to twenty-five knots so they had furled the two gaff sails and put in to the pebble beach for lunch. Maybe reading of Sir Richard Grenfell's career on the Labrador had influenced him. Perhaps it was the mystery of Jennifer's long battle with tuberculosis or his friend Tim's quick death from appendicitis. Maybe these events had left footprints in his subconscious. His father had lifted his eyes from the fire and gazed for several seconds across the wind whipped waves.

"You'll do well," he said, "and we'll all pitch in and be proud."

Often over the years, Matt would recall that moment. Little they knew, on that happy day, that death was just a few months away. His father had died bringing, for the family, a long night of grief and loss. He wept only once; mostly it was a trancelike retracing of events: His father dropping before his eyes, hands unclasping in death, the futile run, walking behind the horse-drawn sleigh on a mild misty morning, the fisherman's band playing '*Nearer My God To Thee*,' the final sound of gravel on wood—'*ashes to ashes …*'

Here was loss indeed—of a father he would never know man to man. He looked down the valley where the Clam brook struggled with spring ice to reach the Mizzen pond. The people sang '*Abide With Me*.'

"I will learn everything," he thought, "I want to know the how and why of life and death."

Clarissa now entered that state only the bereaved know. The fabric of her being had been rent in two and one half discarded. Behind the facial façade lay sadness and memories too private to express; before it was the forced interest in the good intentions and initiatives of neighbours; all but her loss was trivia.

CHAPTER 11

▼

Matt sat on the gunwale of the schooner *Winnifred Bea*, a one hundred and forty ton schooner tied alongside a wharf in St. John's harbour. He doffed his cap to the ship while his eyes did a quick tour of the little vessel. He had one hand on a shroud and a battered suitcase between his legs. Matt closed his eyes and turned his face to the late summer sun. Bird's cries and the smell of hemp and harbour soothed his senses. He thought of the two years of premed at MUN since his dad's death, the journey into the sciences, summer employment at the Bowater paper mill, then the summer past at the Psychiatric Hospital—a plethora of amazing new experiences. In June the letter had arrived saying that he had been accepted into Medical School at Dalhousie University in Halifax, Nova Scotia. His summer was spent in a cocoon of pleasant anticipation, his days spiced with the thrill of the coming challenge. His mother, deprived of her mate, carried on bravely. She had little money and no pension and worried about the cost of Matt's education. Every penny counted. Matt was fortunate to have received a scholarship for the first two years of training and supplemented this by working each summer and the Christmas holidays. Now, through friends, he had obtained free passage on a schooner carrying fish from St. John's to Halifax. Another departure. For the first time he was leaving home for a new country.

Someone jumped down on deck and he looked up to see a lean bearded face staring at him.

"And who are you?"

"Matt Shipman, sir."

"Oh yes, a passenger they said—take a passenger. Well there'll be no passengers on this ship. Consider yourself part of the crew. A student is it? Well, you've got a good name I allows. Shipman I knew, from St. Jones Without 'e was. Good fellar 'e was. Well, c'mon then! Take your gear into the wheelhouse, you'll be lyin' athwart ships, but anything's better than sleeping with that rabble in the fos'cle. By th' way Windsor is the name, Captain Windsor."

The six-man crew tumbled aboard in dribs and drabs, clutching duffle bags and kissing wives and whomever goodbye.

Hours later they were away on a sou'west breeze and just before sunset, he watched in admiration, as the little schooner turned westward around mighty Cape Race. As night fell, the wind backed to the East and increased to gale force. His bunk was a bench behind the steering wheel in the cabin and as she rolled he would slide back and forth, first head then feet hitting the bulkheads.

On deck, the forward watch peered into the darkness from the arrogance of a tiny ship tossing in the turbulence of the sea. His wet arms embraced the bowsprit at the stem head. His body felt each shudder that ran through the ship. Overhead the boomed out convexity of the working jib disappeared into the night. He wiped salt spray from his eyes. Just ahead, the bow light showed the besieging sea, and at intervals, great hissing, sardonic grins of foam rolled by lifting the *Winnifred Bea* and thrusting her sideways.

"Sailor's delight my arse," muttered the lookout, recalling the blood-red sunset now replaced by damp blackness shrieking down from the North East. He felt alone, although just astern, men wrestled with wheel and rope and others swung in hammocks a few feet below. The sea gave another perspective to life; problems and conceits faded in the presence of such powerful indifference. He glanced eastward into the sullen night; two thousand miles away lay Britain and

Europe, licking their wounds. He had never seen England, but blood ties survived the generations.

A figure lurched forward and laid a huge hand on the lookout's shoulder.

"Last fix shows Cape St. Mary's 50 miles off the starboard beam. Keep an eye b'y—I've got a girl in Halifax!"

In the dawn, they found shelter in a fiord, where 500-foot rock walls rose on both sides out of deep water and snaked majestically for miles into the tundra capped southern underbelly of Newfoundland. Here they rode out the storm. Two days later, on a calm, sunny morning, Matt watched Halifax harbour come into view and soon shipped ashore, lugging his brown suitcase and walked up Spring Garden road into the heart of the port city. He had arrived. A sense of permanence and knowing emanated from vine-covered walls. How privileged he was in this oasis of knowledge: students and professors and visiting academics; a connection with famous centers of learning; higher learning that overcame all boundaries of race and colour, uniting homo sapiens in the culture of knowledge, the opportunity to learn about the miracle of biology and himself.

CHAPTER 12

▼

The lecture theatre sloped down to a lectern behind which stood a tall, thin-faced man, stooped slightly from a lifetime of looking down at books. He stroked his goatee and then raised his hand. The rustling of students subsided.

"Ladies and gentlemen." Imagine being called a gentleman. "There is no greater opportunity, responsibility, or obligation given an individual than that of serving as a physician, with the objectives of preventing and curing disease, and relieving suffering of body and mind. Here are our enemies—the causes of disease—slide 1:

> *Infections-*
> > *viral*
> > *fungal*
> > *bacterial*
> > *parasitic*
> > *rickettsial*

> *Neoplasia-*   *benign*
> > *malignant*
> *Trauma*
> *Genetic disorders*

Degenerative-	skeletal, muscular, vascular, etc.
Autoimmune-	mistaken, "friendly fire"
Changes in function-	mainly endocrine disorders
Nutritional	
Psychological-	neurosis, psychosis
Idiopathic	

"These are relentless adversaries that lie in wait during health, injure as disease and inevitably, in the fullness of time cause the destruction of that special biological entity that is life." He then discussed entropy and ethics, closing with a comment on the Physician's role in discussing prognosis with his patient with the quote: "the truth does not justify brutality, and the truth can be brutal."

Arms laden with books, Matt struggled home to his second floor room on Spring Garden Road, which he shared with a laconic Cape Bretoner. The landlady served breakfast, lunch and dinner were at the fraternity house. Mrs. Daley had an obese French poodle and Mr. Daley, who lay on the couch mostly, pale as a waxwork, and said nothing.

Days later, in a macabre ritual, the students were taken to the basement in the Anatomy Building. Here, in a large vat of formalin, floated a dozen or so human bodies, each wrapped in a black shroud. A group of 4 to 5 students selected their own corpse by catching it with a boathook. Later, each group stood around a porcelain table on which the shrouded body lay. Fear and apprehension spread as the black tarpaulin was unwrapped. An arm, blue, mottled in death, was revealed, then the cadaverous face of a middle-aged female. They would all become closely attached to Betsy. The dissection began.

CHAPTER 13

▼

A few months later, Matthew had settled in. Familiarity cast a friendly glow on parks and pathways, library and lecture rooms. The Fraternity house was the favoured center, where singing and camaraderie on weekends subsided to silent lamps shining on textbooks during the week: physiology, biochemistry, anatomy, pharmacology. Sometimes the constant walls closed in and he longed for the freedom of autumn's past. He especially remembered those days when autumn and winter embraced, when branches laden with the first soft, moist whiteness bent toward the russets of leaves and needles on the autumn floor; when the red squirrel, now sleek and winter furred, flied the snow disdainfully, and with vexed commentary, searched for summer seeds. He remembered the quick, dark dive of the loon, surreal in the lake's luminosity, and pines standing nonchalantly in green and white. Then later the fingers of ice along the lakeshore—sparkling ice diamonds that changed from particles to waves at the lapping interface.

In this mood, the Public Gardens beckoned. He and his friend Hotten, a laconic, intense, blue-eyed Cape Bretoner who loved words and used them with witty introspection, would sit among lilies and roses and the solace of ducks on a pond and read Omar Khyam, *The Rhyme of the Ancient Mariner*, or Thomas Grey …

> *'Some village Hampden, that with dauntless breast*
> *The little tyrant of his fields withstood;*
> *Some mute inglorious Milton here may rest.*
> *Some Cromwell guiltless of his country's blood.'*

Or Dylan Thomas …

> *'In the sun that is young once only,*
> *Time let me play and be*
> *Golden in the mercy of his means'*

One night in mid-December, he had lain in his bed, warm after a freezing day delivering the pre-Christmas holiday mail. From the radio came an Oxford accent reading, '*A Child's Christmas in Wales*'.

'I could see the lights in the windows of all the other houses on our own hill and hear the music rising from them up the long, steadily falling night. I turned the gas down, I got into bed. I said some words to the close and holy darkness, and I slept.'

Matt wept for the beauty of words.

*   *   *   *

On his first Christmas away from home, Matt, having learned that his clothing was no match for the winter winds on the streets of Halifax, was pleased when his housemate, Andy McFarlane, invited him to his home in central Nova Scotia.

The McFarlane home stood stoically in the centre of a town built on a massive coal deposit extending far down into the Earth's crust. The town had the sombre appearance of one dependent on a resource-based economy, its personality moulded by economic cycles and tragedies, past and potential. Andy's father and eight brothers were miners. Matt was taken down in a rickety lift far into the black depths where he was appalled by the dirt and darkness and incredulous at the courage of the miners. He breathed a sigh of relief when he again saw sunlit space. Amazing what economics causes men to do, he thought, and how fortunate were our ilk to be fishermen.

At Christmas dinner, the miners were hearty, scrubbed clean and imprisoned in white collars. They were a muscular breed. Matt, fresh from a lecture on inhalation lung diseases, imagined black lungs beneath white shirts. Warmth and hilarity offset any pensive nostalgia that might otherwise have been present. Matt made one slip at dinner—he asked for the Pope's nose when the turkey was being carved.

"So, the Pope's nose is it? And what part of the bird would that be?"

Matt's face reddened. "Oh! Pardon me, it's the—ah—tail end of the turkey—it's also known as the Parson's nose," he added quickly. Roars of laughter followed this.

"Nice try!" said Russell, a huge man now standing over Matt to the great merriment of the rest, "and what kind of a black protestant would you be?"

"Anglican," sputtered Matt, "but not serious."

"Anglican! Church of England! Sure you should be asking for Henry the Eighth's nose, and a large helping that would be!"

Someone began singing '*Henry the Eighth I am, I am*' and all joined in. After much ribaldry, it was decided that Matt would have to wash the turkey pot. Then they drank and sang and the house was hot from bodies, candles and the hissing fire. Collars and vests were loosened and light and music poured out into the white streets. Matt produced his copy of Thomas's '*A Child's Christmas in Wales*' and he and Andy read to an appreciative and satiated audience.

CHAPTER 14

▼

Back at University, Matthew and Karl Hadar decided they would treat themselves by going to hear the Symphony Orchestra. Karl had money because he was a war veteran and Matthew had stopped buying beer and hot sandwiches for two weeks.

Mozart and Strauss, the brochure said, excerpts from *Capriccio* and *Piano Concerto No. 21*. They sat entranced in the warm decor as the orchestra tuned up. Then swelling applause as the Conductor appeared. Someone sat next to Matthew. Through his peripheral vision, he saw two thighs, long, smooth and perfect in symmetry, disappearing beneath a black velvet skirt. His spirits floated with the vitality of Strauss. He saw her legs move and occasionally a white, ring-less hand rested between them. There was fragrance. Physiological things were happening.

At intermission, Matthew nudged Karl and they watched as she walked away, tall, slim, hips forward with a slightly prancing gait.

"Wow!" said Matthew.

"Sure looks like a gynacoid pelvis to me," said Karl.

"Ships that pass in the night," muttered Matthew.

"Oh, c'mon. You want to know who she is? Not a problem. Follow me but stay a few feet away unless I beckon."

They followed into the foyer. The girl was with an older woman, no doubt her mother. They talked for a moment, then the girl joined the bar line-up. Karl walked up to the woman who wore pearls, a grey fur-trimmed coat and a distinguished look.

"Beg your pardon madam," said Karl, "forgive me, but I'm a medical student asked to do a survey on a few of the patrons here. Would you mind just a brief question?"

Karl was tall, moustached, and confident, with a ready smile. He had been a captain in the Canadian army during the Battle of the Schut estuary, and it showed.

"Oh, well, of course," the lady replied.

"Are you from the City or a rural area?"

"Oh, the city! We live on Trafalgar Street on the Arm," she added proudly. "Oh, here comes Linda. Dear, this young man is a medical student. Linda is also at the University studying religion and psychology."

Linda nodded and smiled faintly. Expressive eyes, blond hair and an English complexion.

Karl waved to Matthew.

"I'd like to introduce my friend, Matthew Penwell, also in medicine."

"I'm Clara and this is my daughter, Linda Higgins," said the mother.

"Linda is in psychology," said Karl.

Matthew had difficulty with word flow, but managed, "How nice. We take psychology next term. Maybe we'll see each other then."

"Well, we must go," said Karl, after he had asked a few questions as to how they enjoyed the performance, appraised the changes in the theatre, etc.

"Thank you so much and sorry to bother." Matthew bowed awkwardly and they left.

"You're lucky I'm tied up, Penwell, or you wouldn't get within a gunshot of that one."

"Thanks," Matthew said, in awe, "I owe you one."

During the Mozart half of the concert, Linda and Matt exchanged smiles and said goodnight at the end. It was a different city that Matthew walked home in that night.

The next morning a snowy postman brought a letter from Heart's Content.

Dear Matt,

Just came in from the Bay. We got 8 turrs. A few seals were bobbing among the ice pans.

Dad is slowing down so Tom is going to take over the boats and traps. It's really in his blood. Hey, it's in my blood too but Mr. Dawe says I'm good in mathematics and they've raised some money to send me to Memorial. Also, Granddad had insurance for $500.00.

I was reading about Niels Bohr, Einstein and the scientists that discovered the hydrogen bomb. Some interesting! Mr. Dawe says I should study science.

Hope you are doing well. Not much to report here boy. We chase the girls a bit but the grassin' is long over now in this weather.

We got a few partridge in October—now helping Dad with the wood.

Tom bought a guitar from our cousin Sid in Boston and thinks he's Nashville bound.

All the best,

Jonathan

Matthew nurtured the image of the girl at the symphony. It was sustenance in down times, like a sheet anchor to windward, like a mysterious Christmas present that lay unopened.

"How's your surface anatomy coming along Shipman?" Karl would wink. "Jesus Newf, do I have to hold your hand?"

Mother Nature would not allow indefinite dithering and the chase was on.

They met leaving a psychology lecture and chatted. He walked her to the bus station. He phoned two days later, hesitantly. It went well. She seemed happy and outgoing. Then a week later Linda phoned inviting him to play golf on the weekend. Matt had hardly heard of golf so it was decided he would caddy.

It was spring and it was perfect. Spring green among the dark conifers. Gentle hills, flowers, birds and clouds rolling eastwards—his role to watch this wonderful female—her stance, her walk, her swing. Hear her laugh. He was alive with anticipation.

They met several times for coffee and talked often on the phone, each contact enhancing that special euphoria of growing attraction.

Weeks later, on a moist May night near term's end, Linda and Matt left the Fraternity House and walked down to the sea.

"Follow me," she had said with a beckoning smile and flashed a small key in her palm. "My friend is away for the weekend," she whispered, opening the door marked 4 in the apartment building. Inside it was warm. The sitting room glowed with light reflected off the water. They embraced as soon as the door closed. The world became a torrent of pleasure, each exquisite moment eliminating past and future. Evolution's fabulous trap was sprung in sensuous, frantic knowing. No ism or need could intervene. The zenith of intimacy, the pinnacle of emotional consciousness, was scaled. Afterwards, the holding, the togetherness. He watched the light undulate on the ceiling. She sat up, eyes moist, with a look of troubled joy.

"What's wrong?"

"Oh, maybe I'm feeling a little guilty."

"Why would you? It's natural, it's wonderful!"

"God says this is wrong."

"God doesn't say it's wrong, men do, and for a reason. How could God say something was wrong that he had made so exquisite?"

"You don't have to confess."

He opened a pocket flask of whiskey, which had proven to be unnecessary, and they sat side-by-side, warm, sipping, touching.

"You don't believe," she said. "You're caught in the science thing."

"I love you," he said. "I don't like to see you troubled at this wonderful moment."

"Is it wrong?"

"No, it isn't wrong. You could say it was irresponsible maybe, like if the baby thing happened, but not wrong."

He felt amazement that some outside force could intervene on such intimacy.

He watched her dress. They walked hand in hand through the night. A tiny red signal had been missed. How strange life was. She would be part of his life until he left the port city after graduation. They enjoyed each other's company. Coffee and movies, night skies and walks by the sea. But when intimacies occurred, she fought a battle between conscience and passion. His own exposure to religion had been light-hearted and based on people vaguely following a code of conduct rather than subservience to a creed. He felt her total devotion and dependence on church doctrine. What a powerful first writing on the tabula Rasa! The innocence of childhood was in the hands of men, of priests, to mould. What a responsibility they had, and what a crime if they were wrong.

Linda finally persuaded Matt to visit the Bishop in his palace. Matt walked through streets lined by modest houses of the poor and up imposing steps to an oak door. A woman servant answered and escorted him to a waiting room, richly furnished and decorated with religious art.

"Ah yes, you are Linda Higgins' friend. She spoke of you. What religion are you, Matthew?"

The priest, red-faced and heavy, sat with hands clasped on a green tabletop.

"I was brought up Church of England, sir."

"And you wish to learn about Catholicism so your relationship with Linda may proceed?"

There was a pause.

"I can't believe that religion could blight the love between two people. Is it not more earthly than heavenly power?" Matthew heard himself say.

"The Lord decrees and we obey, my boy."

"I like to think and enquire about things," said Matthew.

"The church is full of great thinkers, great minds that discuss, but agree on the grace of God."

"Science proceeds by trial and error," said Matthew. "The church proceeds by error and trial." He couldn't believe his impertinence. It just came out.

The Bishop laughed, looking suddenly like an old Dickensonian rogue, and clasped his hands on his ample stomach.

"Science confuses itself very often. You are destined, I'm sure, to go through the Darwinian wilderness, but there is a way out. Here, my boy, take this book and read it if you will. Then if you wish to talk further …"

"Thank you," Matthew said. They smiled at each other and Matthew was escorted out.

His steps were light on the pavement. He felt a thrill of freedom, of good fortune, of the treasure of books and knowledge that lay unfettered before him.

How had he escaped this powerful ubiquitous force designed to control and shape the human brain at its most vulnerable? A force so overwhelming: born of an all-powerful God, proclaimed by such entrenched hierarchies, aided and abetted by parents whom we trust above all, decorated with beautiful words, music, art, overwhelming architecture, rituals and finally trumped by the grand bribe prize of everlasting joy in Heaven, or threat of unending agony in Hell, if one dissents. "This is either true," he thought, "or the greatest crime imaginable!"

He climbed the stairs to his room and lay in the dark. "How does religion fit into evolution?" he thought. "Binding together. Sensing strength in numbers. Following the most capable leader. Did this increase the chance of survival? Was this an advantage and is it still? Is someone who doesn't think beyond the frame of religion not comforted in this life so vulnerable to time and fate?"

The Lord is my shepherd, I shall not want. He leadeth me beside the still water ...'

And he slept.

They met once after he had moved, a rendezvous in a dark December town. There was sadness in their intimacy.

'Their thirst and longing could not rise above the barrier of reason'—*The White Cliffs* by Alice D. Miller.

Both had within, a passion greater than their love. The music stopped.

CHAPTER 15

▼

In the autumn of his first year at Dalhousie, Matt had joined the Naval Cadets, University Naval Training Division, at HMCS *Stadacona*. Stewart McAllister, a classmate, joined with him. McAllister was an ex-serviceman. He was balding, with small bright eyes in a face always on the brink of laughter and pale with a permanent five o'clock shadow. His head was mostly tipped up because he was short and used to looking up at people. He was a rascal on the edge and headed for trouble. His buddies intervened at times, but he held his course toward the rocks. They passed the medical, received gear, and were scheduled to 'come aboard' when the University year ended. It was announced that after basic training they would be on a voyage to England.

July 5, 1949

Dear Jonathan,

I'm writing from the mess deck of the Destroyer HMCS Crescent. Lat 43 50' N, Long 4 13'W, course 096 (I just came down from the bridge). We left Halifax 2 days ago. Just as the land disappeared, a British Cruiser appeared out of the mist, all flags flying, and we fired a Royal Salute, as it was the

Queen's birthday. Captain ordered 'splice the main brace'
which means a tot of rum for everyone. In an hour it was grey
and gusting and most of the Canadian lads were sick; lots of
rum left lying around for the old salts. Very excited about seeing England in a few days. It's great up on the bow as forward
watch. Scanning the sea and feeling her rise and fall. Especially at night, looking astern you see all the lights of a great
ship, like a many-eyed monster plowing through the darkness.
Sure puts one in awe of the men who fought out here during
the War.

That's great news about your going to Memorial. You didn't
seem too smart to me but we'll see! How will the Village get
along without you and me? Tom will have to take care of land
and sea until we get back.

May see you at Christmas if I can't get a job in Halifax.

Cheers,

Matthew

*'The history of England is that of one of mankind's outstanding suc-
cesses. It is the history of how certain Saxon and Danish tribes, isolated on
an island on the outer rim of Europe, merging with Celtic and Roman
survivors and organized by adventurers from Normandy, became, with
the passing centuries, the masters of one third of this planet. It is instruc-
tive to probe the secret of a destiny as fortunate and impressive as that of
ancient Rome ... the strength of the English people springs equally from
the disciplined, fearless, trusting and tenacious character molded by a
thousand years of happy fortune.'*—The Miracle of England by André
Maurois

*'I have loved England, dearly and deeply, since that first morning,
shining and pure. The white cliffs of Dover I saw rising steeply out of the
sea that once made her secure'*—The White Cliffs by Alice D. Miller

Matt's first view of England was the white rocks of the Needles that blended with a mist glowing in the morning sun. How many white ensigns had waved over wakes as ships passed out of the Solent and turned southwest, around the Needles, the most westerly tip of the Isle of Wight? Cook, Drake, Nelson, Chichester, Navies that would probe and chart the farthest sea reaches of the planet—ships returning from victory and defeat, failure and glory.

H.M.S. Crescent came alongside in Portsmouth. Two days later, a euphoric Matthew sat on an English train on the way to London, sipping a pint of bitters and watching the gentle landscape rush by.

The days that followed were a mixture of awe and excitement. He scratched the surface of this amazing nation; its countryside of gentle curvaceous greens where even tropical plants grew; its ferocious coasts where wind and tide had honed the sailors' skills; monuments to democracy, science, literature, justice, adventure and capitalism. The home of sports, tennis, golf, soccer, cricket … a treasure chest that had bequeathed many of the ingredients of civilization to planet Earth. A nation, commonwealth and Empire that recently, standing alone, had sacrificed its treasure in defence of that civilization. What a glorious way to end an empire!

On the last day he visited Cambridge, stood in King's College, read the long list of Nobel Laureates, and vowed that he and Jonathon would return one day.

They had some fun also in London. Prostitutes in Piccadilly Circus were strictly for talking, as they remembered recent lectures in sexually transmitted diseases, although Stewart McAllister had to be pulled away after getting into a fight with a Scotsman over one of the girls. That night they had steak in Soho and then went to the *Follies Bergere* at the London Hippodrome, where they were invited on stage, performed and were given a bottle of champagne. Waiting for the girls at the stage door proved fruitless. Getting back to the Tavistok Hotel very late they overslept, missed the train from Victoria Station to Portsmouth and had to convince a London cabby to drive them to the ship for 26 pounds sterling—a King's ransom! Late getting aboard, they were confined to ship and given slack party duties for three days. Blame it mostly on McAllister.

CHAPTER 16

▼

The second year of Medical school was well underway. The aura of death besieged Matthew's olfactory nerve as he entered the autopsy room. He had been reading the chapter on cranial nerves in Diseases of the Nervous System by Sir Russell Brain, and committing to memory the mnemonics. Eight students sat on elevated benches to the left of the porcelain table, on which lay the body of a man, a 52 year-old who had died of stab wounds on the weekend. Yellow fluorescence, reflecting off white walls, enhanced the early tarnish of putrescence. A power saw, whose circular blade rotated at right angles to the shaft, suddenly screamed in the hands of the resident in Pathology. The sound fell an octave as the blade cut into the skull on a line that would sever a cap of cranium. Careful hands avoided damage to tissues underlying the bone. Sue Manley, pale and perspiring, was helped out but returned in a few minutes. Matthew felt lightheaded but forced himself to breath slowly and it passed.

The bony skullcap was pried off revealing a shiny greyish-white membrane, the dura mater covering the brain. This was inspected, incised and folded back showing the convoluted brain surface covered only by the transparent arachnoid membrane. Using a fine curved knife, the resident severed the twelve cranial nerves and the medulla oblongata, the upper portion of the spinal cord, allowing the brain to be removed and placed on a tray. Before them lay the most advanced structure of biology, the supreme accomplishment of what scientists call, 'Complex Biological Systems'.

"This is the most evolved part," intoned the Resident, pointing to the convoluted surface.

It has the look and colour of ribbed sea sand, thought Matthew, recalling a line from 'The Rhyme of the Ancient Mariner'.

"The cerebral cortex, the grey matter, is made up of 10 billion neurons, each neuron an autonomous unit able to maintain its own metabolism and develop, store, enhance, inhibit, transmit and receive electron messages via as many as 100 connections with its fellow neurons. This incredible living web, seething with electrical messages, is us—literally, our awareness, personalities, our hopes and fears. Every aspect of our consciousness is the result of an electrical event in this neuronal maze, which connects, by nerve outflow in the cranial nerves and spinal cord, to every cell in the body."

He demonstrated the surface anatomy of the cerebral cortex, the cerebellum and medulla oblongata. The brain was then placed in formaldehyde to be preserved for dissection and microscopic examination.

The students left quietly, each subdued in wonder. The mood continued until chairs had been scraped around a coffee table.

"Hey, I lifted the tray, that brain is heavy," said Stewart.

"So, that's us. That's what we are. It seemed so low key lying there, how ignominious. Shouldn't there still be a glow, lights flashing or something?" mused Matt. "It looks like a coral sponge."

"C'mon, Penwell, its dead," said Karl.

"That Resident sounded like a wannabe philosopher," commented Sue, a freckled redhead from P.E.I. "He mentioned everything except the soul, Alex."

Alex Mercer was a Baptist Minister. He was dark, laconic, with always the suggestion of a smile.

"Maybe we'll see the soul under the microscope, Padre," needled Karl.

"Just keep subtracting what you see guys," Alex said, "and when there's nothing left that will be the soul."

There was silence for a moment.

"So we just apply that first lecture, the Causes of Disease, to the brain, then figure out how all these etiologies present clinically. Then, if we remember all the syndromes given the names of old farts, we'll be neurologists," said Tait.

"O.K. you guys," Karl annouced, scraping back his chair. "Party Friday night at the Frat, Irving on the piano—hey, it's just been tuned. B.Y.O.B. Come on, it's time for Pharmacology."

The Fraternity House stood square and gray, on Robie Street. Across a wooden sill, worn by the feet of generations of medical students, opened a foyer filled with boots and coats. Removing the partition between the living and dining rooms had created a large space. A piano and phonograph, along with several deep armchairs, adorned one end, while a large dining room table laboured at the other. The table could be stowed making room for dancing. A dumbwaiter led to the kitchen where Molly the cook reigned. Some seniors had rooms upstairs but most students lived elsewhere though they ate and played at the Frat.

When Matt walked in with Linda, the phonograph was playing Bali High. They were seeing each other on a platonic basis, except for one recent occasion when reason did not prevail. There were a few days of intense anxiety when Linda feared pregnancy but tonight they were celebrating good news and could relax as friends. The place filled with students and their dates. Drinks, songs around the piano, a performance by the Frat barbershop quartet, then dancing and couples gradually disappear as the evening wound down. As they were leaving, Karl approached with a rueful smile.

"Just got a call from McAllister—he's in jail!"

"What? What happened?"

"He was drinking in a taxi and a cop spotted him. At the station, when they interrogated him, he stated that he was a war veteran and asked what they were doing while he was fighting for King and Country—so they locked him up."

"Let's go get 'im."

"No, let him cool his heels. We'll get him in the morning."

Later Matt lay in his bed before sleep and went over his day. "Many things we don't need," he thought, "but we do need friends and music and humour—maybe we even need McAllister."

In the last few weeks before the final exams the medical class turned inward on itself. Social life waned, replaced by anxiety and whiffs of paranoia. Students retreated into notes and books. Lights burned late. Faces paled. Old exam papers were scrutinized. There was too much to know! One must be lucky. Written exams, orals, lab tests, anatomy displays—It all roiled toward the fateful day. Then, sleep deprived and with spastic intestines, they stood waiting for the doors to open, forcing conversation through tight smiles. Now the battle was joined and fear evaporated—from somewhere came the tenacity to write incessantly as the hours passed in a flash.

Then it was over.

Now, in a flood—freedom, camaraderie, spring. Then the final party and dispersal to summer jobs.

Matt was elated. Three weeks before a letter had arrived approving his application for employment with the Newfoundland Department of Health. He was going back to the Great Island and would be Medical Officer for the Labrador Coast aboard the *Winnifred Bea*, a 140-ton schooner, Captain Windsor and a crew of six, leaving St. John's June first.

"I'll be the doctor for all the tiny outports strung along hundreds of miles of Atlantic Coast, Aboriginals and summer fishermen!" he thought, "What a jump from the academic to reality!"

CHAPTER 17

▼

The taxi wound down the dusty road into Southern Cove. Jonathan glimpsed the heart shaped harbour, the familiar hills and ponds, houses clustered along the shore, and the white church dominant on the hill. It was May 12 when Jonathan, having finished first year Engineering, was coming home for the summer.

Rachel, damp of eye, greeted him with a hug, while Sam, an admiring smile on his face, stood in the background a moment before shaking hands.

"B'y you made it back," said Sam. "How was the trip?"

"Long enough for sure. A north wind and lots of pack ice slowed us down on the Gulf of St. Lawrence. I enjoyed the old train though. Stood out on the back platform of the caboose and watched. How many ponds are there that have never been fished! Sure nice to see the southwest arm of Trinity Bay. It's good to be home!"

"I've got moose stew cookin' b'y, the moose your father got in behind Sooley's gullies. Tom'll soon be in from the Bay. Roseanne is working down at Martin's store."

"'E's a little pale around the gills," said Sam, "but a few days fishin' will fix that."

"So are you settled in this new place?" asked Jonathan.

"Yes b'y, peoples' nice, even the richees on the hill, and we get a Doctor twice a week and Minister every fortnight." said Rachel.

"Well, I misses the old cove and me trap berth. Lard Jasus, it was isolated but I hates the thought of not dyin' there," said Sam.

"Your friend Matt Penwell is coming tomorrow. E's a doctor near enough now people say, and you a part engineer! Dat's great my son! You got to tell us some of dat stuff you're learnin', though we be too stupid to understand no doubt!" added Rachel.

C H A P T E R   18

▼

Eastwards towards home; the gray restless gulf, train huffing through the Topsail Mountains, central lakes and tundra, then the Avalon Peninsula and villages by the sea.

Matt was startled. His mother seemed so small and fragile to his embrace. She had been widowed for five years and carried the sadness of memory only the bereaved can know. Also, the village society had collapsed back on its fisherman base leaving her nostalgic for the old days when the outport had been a bustling center of communication between Europe and America. They had afternoon tea and talked for a long time.

"The Deaconess has offered me a role at the Anglican Orphanage in St.John's."

"Really! Great, Mom I'm sure that would be good for you."

"There's nothing left for me here now," she said, "I can't think of the old days without tears! Oh, by the way, Jonathan is back and said he wanted to see you soon as he could. They say he won a scholarship. His family bought the old Mallam home."

A land breeze pushed tiny wavelets toward the coloured west as Matt approached the Shipman house. A net lay along the fence and a turned down skiff adorned the front lawn where 'piss-a-beds' posed, triumphant after the change of owners.

Inside, people sat along kitchen walls or stood in doorways—children, grammas, dogs. There was spruce beer on the table and the aroma of salt cod came from a colander in the sink. A roar went up when Matthew arrived.

"Here's Matt, 'e's a Doctor now, mostly, isn't 'e. My son, we could sure use you 'ere."

"We're going to sing a song. Matt can sing. Let's 'ear you Matt."

The pump organ, fiddle and accordion struck up and all hands sang:

> *"The next comes the Doctor*
> *The worst case of all*
> *He says, what's the matter with you all the fall*
> *He says he can cure you of all your disease*
> *When he gets all your money*
> *You can die if you please*
> *And it's hard, hard times"*

Roars of laughter followed this chorus. They danced, sang and talked at a decibel level Matthew had forgotten. Jonathan and Matthew, shouting over the din, arranged to go salmon fishing the next day. Matt walked back along the rocky lane with a lingering taste of spruce beer and moist eyes as he hummed the last song:

> *Let me view that rugged shore*
> *Where the beach is all a glissen*
> *With the caplin spawn where from dusk to dawn*
> *You bait your trawl and listen*
> *To the undertow a hissin'*
>
> *When I reach that last big shoal*
> *Where the ground swells break asunder,*
> *Where the wild sands roll to the surges toll*

Let me be a man and take it
When my dory fails to make it.

—'*Let me fish off Cape St. Marys*'
by Otto P. Kelland

He was home.

CHAPTER 19

▼

Tom towed the small sloop to the harbour mouth where a light breeze cats-pawed off the cliffs.

"I'll cast y'es off 'ere my sons, you'll likely be in the same spot when I gets back," chuckled Tom. "Try y'er luck on Freshwater brook."

Jonathan and Matthew set sail along the coast, where the sea shone emerald just before breaking white on the shore. They sailed a few miles watching sea birds and occasionally a seal or the rolling dark humpback whales chasing herring in the bay. Approaching Seal Cove, they were headed by the wind. They skulled the last few yards and tied on to a stick protruding from a shelving rock that had a miniature harbour to seaward. Crossing the pebble beach, they followed a moose trail up a clay bank from which they could see rapids flowing into a pool overhung by spruce and balsam.

On the first cast, Jonathan was sure he saw water whelm. The next time the silver doctor touched the surface, there was a splash—a flashing shape leaped out of the water and the battle was on. In five minutes, a four-pound salmon lay glistening on the moss. Soon, black flies drove them back to the beach where they boiled the kettle and sat in a sensory cocoon of forest perfume, wood smoke, the green of new growth, subtle shades on the sea, and the calming cadence of rolling pebbles.

"Isn't this something!" exuded Matt.

"Boy, bottle this for your patients, it would fix 'em up."

"You're right. We seem to have evolved a striving that brings with it the scourge of anxiety."

"And the more we separate ourselves from the natural things, the worse it gets, it seems," said Jonathan.

"Maybe the happiest time was in the Garden, when Adam and Eve had lots to gather and not much in the way of competition."

"Nature does seem to have a calming effect, even when she gets temperamental. Maybe hunter-gatherer societies were the happiest."

"Sounds great if you aren't being hunted or gathered," mused Matt. "Changing the subject just a little, any luck with the girls in St. John's?"

"No, boy. Well, I went steady with a redhead for almost a year. She was in nursing. We had good times. Then she got sick with the measles. Tim, a friend of mine, had the measles also. I didn't put two and two together. A little later, she wrote me a letter saying she's fallen for Tim and goodbye. I felt a little petulant at first, but my buddies laughed so hard and so long that I had to join in and have been laughing at it ever since. How about you?"

"Yeah, a nice one in Halifax but she's too religious."

"I didn't think that would matter today."

"Don't kid yourself. That's something else we've got to figure out; the tendency for Human beings to believe something in the absence of evidence or proof."

Jonathan poked the ashes with an alder stick. He watched as light flared and smoked curled past the blackened kettle.

"Why is it that the animal with the big brain is the most screwed up?"

"People believe weird things."

"And they don't just nibble—they'll swallow some bizarre idea whole."

"Often someone has set our dials before we know what's happening."

"If man could become part of a great quest to understand the universe and himself—the nuts and bolts of what and who he is—what makes him tick—his place in biology—don't you think that would alter his behaviour?"

They watched as a sea otter ran along the beach, stopped a few feet away, stared for many seconds and then, rushed off.

"Hey, this is great, you coming to Halifax. We have discussions every couple of weeks; philosophers, psychologists, scientists … it's terrific. I'll keep you up on biology and medicine and you can help me with physics. There are so many great questions, so thrilling to know. How about it?"

"Sounds great," said Jonathan. "I'm just a beginner, but it's very exciting. Hey, I was just reading what happened the year you were born."

"What happened in 1930?"

"Wolfgang Pauli discovered the neutrino."

"What's a neutrino?"

"It's a subatomic particle with no electric charge and no mass. They spin. They go through the world without touching it. They can go through a lead shield many light years thick."

"Whoa," said Matt, "Enough already. You're going to have to start at the beginning."

"Then there's antimatter, also first conceived in 1930 by Paul Divac."

"Antimatter?"

"Yes b'y, everything has its opposite, like an electron has its antiparticle, the positron. When the two meet, they annihilate each other."

"Ok, sorry I asked. Save it for Halifax. Oh, I just found the 'Origin of Species' by Charles Darwin that I plan to read on the voyage north."

"Hey, there's a sea eagle and she's got a fish."

They watched water sparkle from the doomed fish held fore and aft for maximal aerodynamic effect. A boat came around the point.

"Well, let's ask the big questions and see if we can find some answers," mused Jonathan.

"Ok, like, how did we get here, for starters?"

"There is a great ferment out there. As we sit here, there are thousands of scientists working at every imaginable project. Imagine, all over the Planet, thousands—maybe hundreds of thousands of our brightest minds—in thousands of Universities and Research facilities, studying every aspect of our Universe."

"And studying for the sake of truth, of knowing."

"And it is self-policing; every idea and hypothesis is subject to the critique of fellow scientists which prevents power grabbing by pseudo scientists. Imagine, a huge machine producing the facts of our existence!"

"Science eliminates the boundaries of family, tribe, nation and race. That's what I like."

"Great," said Jonathan, standing. "Salmon for supper. Let's go. My head's getting fuzzy."

"It's the spruce beer."

Jonathan collected the plates and walked down to the water's edge. The westering sun was still warm on his face. He went down on his haunches and took a handful of wrinkled sand and was startled when a crab scuttled away from his touch. He was about to take a second handful when he stopped. Partially uncovered was a yellowish structure and, as he looked, the next tiny wave removed more of the sand revealing what looked like a human hand. Jonathan drew back, dropping a plate.

"Hey Matt, come here! Look what I've found!"

Matt looked for a moment then carefully brushed away more sand.

"Must be a seal flipper," said Jonathan, "they look just like humans."

"No," said Matt slowly, "that's a human hand." He gently cleared more sand, tugged on the bone and out came a skeletal hand with attached forearm bones, the elbow joint and a humerus that was broken off halfway along the shaft.

"Look. There's a bracelet on the wrist!"

They stared at the metal chain attached to an oval plate, both showing only rust, then at each other with a silent surmise; another a story had merged with theirs.

"Well, we'll have to mark the spot and take the bones to the police. Can't leave them here, the animals would take them. Let's have a look around."

Nothing unusual was found along the beach or the adjacent sea-bed. Carefully they placed the skeletal remains on a towel laid on blackberry moss in the fore-cuddy, next to the shining salmon.

The boat sailed home on the evening offshore breeze with a sober crew wondering about the mystery of the bones in the sand.

CHAPTER 20

▼

It was late summer in Heart's Content. The cycles of salmon, lobster and capelin had all passed and the new murrs were long fledged and flying on Baccalieu Island. Rachel opened the creaking gate, disturbing a brown middle-aged mutt who rushed out of an aging doghouse with an angry bark that changed suddenly into tail wagging recognition. The yard contained remnants of summer blooms—marigolds, nasturtiums and struggling shrubs poking up between lobster pots, an old fish net and odds and ends of boards left over from last winter's skiff building. The house was a square two-story clapboard structure painted deep blue and recently touched up.

Opening the door, she felt a brush of air laden with kitchen odours and heard glass clinking. Her neighbour, Jane Trepanier, was fishing bottles out of a large steaming pot. She wore an apron over a loose cotton dress that was buttoned unevenly at the neck. Saturday morning curlers in her hair suggested a weird metallic hat pressing down on deep-set blue eyes, high cheekbones and a perspiring face.

"Here you are—c'mon in. Wish they would stop bringing home rabbits, but no, it's rabbits, rabbits, rabbits! Got no choice but to bottle some. C'mon in, I'll put on the kettle."

"Tea would be nice," said Rachel, sitting down at the kitchen table, "sure I wanted to hear about your trip upalong."

Jane wiped her hand in her apron and found a spot for the kettle on the crowded woodstove.

"My dear what an experience! I was like a child sure, some excited; from the moment I put down five dollars for the car ride to St. John's. Then it was train to Port Au Basque, boat across the gulf and another day and a half on the train to Toronto. Not much sleep."

"Stayed with your cousin in Toronto did you?"

"Yes—right downtown—some busy. Walking distance from the bus station and the big hotel—the Royal something it's called. Helen is kind a wild ..." Jane lowered her voice, "but of course she's much younger." She got up and closed the hall door. Her face was intent and her hands accompanied her voice. "We went to a place one night—a bar they called it—my dear! Music! Flashing lights like you've never seen. Anyway, we had a drink—I had rye and something. Then these two guys wanted to dance. Well this went on and the next thing I knew Helen was gone. My mind got all confused. Anyway, the fellar finally took me home. You can get carried away you know—but nothing really happened I'm sure. I kept thinking of Selwyn. What would he do and say if he knew? Anyway nothing really happened." Jane put a hand on Rachel's shoulder, "but I was glad to see the red tide a few days ago!" She sat down, slapped her thighs, and laughed. "Mind this is only for your ears and mine."

"Of course my dear—most of it seems like fun."

Jane got up and poured the tea, then covered the pot with a large sealskin cozy.

"That red tide," said Rachel, "would you believe I didn't get mine last month—can't believe I'm pregnant."

"Oh my dear! How are you feeling? Any changes up here?" Jane lifted her ample breasts.

"No, I just feel tired. But it can't be. Sam and I weren't at it for the last two months."

"Nothin' for two months! That would be a famine for my Selwyn—no way I could get away with that."

Rachel looked at the rain tracing crooked paths down the misted panes.

"It's not Sam, it's me. I can't believe how things have changed from the early years when it was here, there and everywhere and everyone having a whale of a time. For the past year I could care less."

"How old are you?" Jane's expression had changed to concern from the flushed excitement of her Canadian story.

"Thirty-nine."

"That's what I thought—way too early—although it happens I suppose. It happened to Sadie Cornish over in the cove but she had some other problems I'm told—medical it was."

"I'm okay, except for being tired and some arthritis, mostly hands and knees. I'll wait a bit and then go and see the Doctor."

Jane started to speak, but was interrupted by a shout from the yard. Selwyn, a stout figure with robust countenance, entered wearing oilskins and a cape ann.

"Can't get that old coker to go," he said, "just like the song. B'y it sure rained but now she's only peckin' down." He gave Rachel a hug. She felt the damp cold of oilskins and the male heat underneath.

"Did old Sam get any cod this mornin'?"

"Not back yet," said Rachel, looking up at the kitchen clock with the green carved cuckoo. "Great to see you both. I must run home and get something for dinner."

CHAPTER 21

▼

St. John's lay astern bathed in a purplish glow born of the twilight sky and reflections from the lustrous sea. The city looked like a jewel, sparkling in the center of a giant Henry Moore, chiselled from the darkening sea-girt cliffs that rose majestically on either side of the narrows.

Matt stood at the taffrail, feeling the diesel throb and watching the wake pour astern like a white finger pointing to what had been. Light reflecting softly off the bandage of low cloud gave a halo effect over the receding city. The memory of old ships was in the air: fishing fleets, gray warships, the joy of shelter and the thrill of a dangerous unknown. He smiled as a rhyme from childhood crossed his mind—a poem by Charles E. Carryl:

> 'The night was thick and hazy
> When the Piccadilly Daisy
> Carried down her crew and Captain in the sea,
> And I guess she must have drowned 'em
> For they never ever found 'em
> And I know they didn't swim ashore with me.'

Guess I'm planning to be another Robinson Crusoe, he chuckled to himself. Shouldn't I be more profound at this time? Maybe poetry was a way to interface between two solitudes—the land and sea, science and the arts. Poetry had one foot in the structural precision of words and another in the freedom of metaphor: a junction between the explicit and the aesthetic in human consciousness.

He watched as Signal Hill passed to port and the schooner bore northward across Cuckold Cove. A shy three-quarter moon rose towards Ireland and Venus was bright astern. The light waned quickly but an iceberg grounded on Cape Spear still glowed a mysterious opalescence. He thought of the past few days. Rumour and speculation had spread through the village. The bones were taken to Jonathan's house. The police officer, Dan Gosse, was visiting his mother on the south coast. They finally contacted the Criminal Investigation Department in St. John's. Tom and his boat had been hired to explore the sand and sea in the area of the find.

The dental course in St. John's had been reduced to one day, as the dentist failed to appear. On that last day, he had gone to the General Hospital where he met a florid, elderly dentist in the emergency department. A man, who was serving a life sentence for murder, was brought in and Dr. Gross demonstrated the pulling of a tooth, then handed the forceps to Matt. He recalled the anxiety. The trick was to get a proper hold on the tooth; just push the jaws of the forceps a little farther down below the gum line, now squeeze, then a firm strong pull with a slight twist, and suddenly there was a give and the long yellow tooth was out.

The next day was spent checking and storing supplies; surgical and dental instruments, splints and bandages, several bottles of medicinal brandy—the latter of special interest to the crew, then a last visit with friends who brought him aboard at 10:00 p.m. Suddenly it was cold. He shivered, took a last look around at the falling night, and went below.

> *Dawn found them sailing on the insouciant sea*
> *Guests in the sea god's realm*
> *Of currents and ebb tides,*

Of foggy shrouds and peevish winds
When Poseidon and Proteus employ
Shoals and eternal shores
To punish hubris or humility

They sailed all morning through a choppy, quartering sea. Mid afternoon, Matt was on deck with Skipper Jim peering into a dense fog, visibility about 75 yards. The schooner powered slowly, wallowing in the restless waves. The sun's light, absorbed in the fog, threw a peculiar glow over the whole scene.

Captain Windsor was at the wheel and worried. The log showed that Cape John must be near, but had the current swept her off course? The four old skippers, passengers to Labrador, gathered on the fos'cle discussing the situation. At 3:25 p.m., Matt became vaguely aware of a different sound coming out of the fog.

"Do you hear anything unusual?" He asked Skipper Andrew, who was leaning over the rail and peering into the mist.

"No, b'y. I hears only the bow wave, but these are old ears I'm carrying around."

Matt listened intently. Suddenly there was no doubt. He had heard water sluicing dead ahead. He rushed aft to the wheelhouse and shouted a warning. Captain Windsor went hard a starboard and reversed the engine. Then they saw it. A large white apparition in the iridescent mist. Iceberg! They easily cleared the Greenland monster and then resumed course at a slow speed. In seconds, just as the iceberg faded into the mist off their port quarter, came a shout from the bow lookout.

"Breakers, Breakers!" and where fog met the sea appeared the ominous image of foam on rocks.

"Hard a starboard!" yelled Captain Windsor, as he flung the wheel over and cut power. The breakers grinned and beckoned. It was all geometry now. The moving radius of a circle. They waited for the crunch, the schooner's moan of distress, but then the foam was astern and they breathed again.

"Lucky there were no rocks to port or we'd be in the soup now," murmured Skipper Dan.

The rest of the afternoon, they crawled along the shore, sounding the horn to get an echo from the cliffs. With darkness, they would stand out to sea, but suddenly the schooner broke out of the fog and they saw the lighthouse on Bear point. Passing between high cliffs into the harbour, the *Winnifred Bea* broke into bright sunlight and eased alongside the jetty. How quickly the scene changes.

"There's where we were b'y," Skipper Tim said, pointing a gnarled finger to Cape John on the chart. "What a place to drown—nothin' 'der but desolation and the devil throwin' rocks at it."

Matt spruced up and set off for the Cottage Hospital that served this port on the N.W. coast of Bonavista Bay. Nurse Cairns warmly greeted him and they chatted while waiting for Dr. Eamon Murphy and nurse Humby, who had gone fishing.

"Sure 'tis glad we are to see you. Come along while I clean a few trout and we'll have a feed for supper. How's the *Winnifred Bea*?" Murphy was tall, freckled and had greying red hair.

"You're just in time," he continued, "tomorrow it's boat to Pool's Island, about 24 miles, so you'll get to know the territory."

"So you're from Ireland!" said Matt "Is it orange or green?"

"Ah, 'tis green for sure—one of those Catholic Republicans you've heard about."

"It sure is ongoing over there."

"Well, we never quite escaped the English you see. Never got 'em off our backs."

They feasted on speckled trout and crab legs with partridgeberry pie for dessert. Sitting before the fire, they watched the light cavort through brandy snifters.

"Unfortunately for the Irish, they lived next to the Anglo Saxons, who would incredibly become masters of one-quarter of the globe," said Matt. "The Irish became an obstacle they tripped over every time they left home looking for a more exotic clime. Like running aground as soon as you cast off."

"They didn't trip. They stepped on us, and we helped them. For the love of Jesus, we fought for their Empire!"

Matt considered his next line. "Ah ... maybe indeed your troubles are all because of the English. Any other race would have obliterated such an ankle biter, but the Englishman's sense of fair play prevented the final solution."

Murphy sipped his brandy and his complexion seemed a little redder.

"They did very bad things to us; took our land, made us peasants and let us starve. Fair play indeed! We owe them nothing."

"Except maybe part of your literature," murmured Matt, knowing he had gone too far.

Dr. Murphy slapped his knee.

"Look here Penwell. You're an agent provocateur! A few years ago, I'd be challenging you to a duel, but I am enjoying this in some perverse way. Go ahead and hit me again."

"Well," said Matt, "Begging your pardon and thanking you as a gracious host, it seems to me that you've been badly abused by history, but you compounded the injuries from the English by retreating into the arms of Catholicism which put the blinders on you ever since."

"I think I like you Penwell, but you could be missing after tomorrow's trip. The church is a double-edged sword, I'll admit, but I don't think it holds a society back as much as you think. Most of us never rise above the need for solace. Those that fancy themselves smart can be intellectual and scientific and still fall back on the church when the going gets rough—as it will. There's no need to mix science and religion. They are at opposite ends of consciousness."

"Ah, consciousness. A great word," replied Matt. "I'm most interested in that; what is it and how sustained?"

"You've been too long on the *Winnifred Bea*," Murphy commented. "I've been alone too long here. It's lonely medically, and that's why I was looking forward to your visit. Now I'm not sure—a bloody Orangeman probably. Oh, by the way, I want you to meet

Father Raoul Cyr. He's always good for a meal and a Cuban cigar. He's a Frenchman—another race abused by the English—it goes on and on."

He stood up and put a log on the fire. The balsam burned furiously. "Let's have a little music before bed." He put a 45 record on the turntable. The first notes enthralled Matt: he had never heard Wagner before—the overture to *Tannhauser.* The music ebbed and flowed, entwined with this special day and enhanced his mood. He listened, spellbound, while the acoustic beauty overwhelmed. When silence reigned, they stood, shook hands and, eschewing words that might break the spell, Matt retired to his bed.

Diary June 8ᵗʰ, 1952

Awake at 5 a.m. and boarded motorboat at Badger's Quay. Weather 'mauzy'. Arrived Pool's Island 9 a.m. Sarah Dowling, age 9, abdominal pain. Dr. Murphy diagnosed appendicitis and I agree. Arrangements for hospitalization. Bill Steele, congestive heart failure. 10 patients in all. Return voyage 12 noon. Choppy off Shoe Cove point. Terns. Icebergs. Shearwaters. Ptarmigan dinner with Father Cyr. Assisted at appendectomy. Discussed Darwin. Made calls in the village. Gout and renal failure. Rex drove me back aboard at 1 a.m. What responsibility he has! Humour intrinsic in the people. Impressed. And so to bed.

CHAPTER 22

▼

Four days later they were trapped in Arctic ice. The coast of Labrador could sometimes be seen miles to the west. A few inches from the crew, as they slept in their bunks, was an unimaginable force, while below lurked the cold beauty of the water of the Arctic current dropping 100 fathoms to the bottom and filled with the life cycles of aquatic biology. It was remarkable really—the ship's hull was like a robin's egg in a huge vice. The most dangerous time was when they were first trapped, and the skipper had all hands on deck with long poles trying to fend off and position the pans relative to the hull. Once the trap was complete, the ice arrangement around the hull fended off other ice and the forces were static. It was when movement was present that danger was extreme, as it would be when the field began to break.

Matt slept. Thought. Studied the anatomy of the inferior dental nerve. Read from Palgrave's *Treasury of Verses, The Voyage of the Beagle* and John Ruskin's *Ethics of the Dust.* On sunny days, they played ball on huge ice pans and suntanned. The crew's clamour for medicinal brandy was irresistible. Those weekday rogues became pious on Sundays. At 11:00 a.m. everyone gathered around the radio in the fos'cle, clean shirts and bareheaded, to hear the Sunday Service from V.O.C.M. in St. John's. The sound waxed and waned, assaulted by cosmic radiations that produced great snaps and crackles. But it wasn't the message so much as a chance to join in the hymns.

'Jesus Saviour pilot me', *'For all the Saints who from their labours rest'*; their voices lost quickly in the endless expanse of ice.

The cook, who was suffering mightily from enforced celibacy, served Sunday dinner—turrs that had been shot off the bow and retrieved with a dip net, potatoes, turnip and hard tack. After dinner, they wouldn't play games, because it was the Lord's Day.

"Tell us a story, Skipper Jim. You're some good at dat b'y."

"Well," Skipper Jim smiled, tamping tobacco into his pipe and reaching for a match, "It's a rough lookin' crowd you are, and all of us in a strange place. I allows the doctor can tell the best story as 'es the only one of this lot that's got learnin'."

"C'mon skipper!"

A sudden squall, the hull creaked and the rigging hummed a low note.

"Well, d'eres somethin' been botherin' me for years and I likes to talk about it. The schooner *Blackduck,* out of Fortune," he paused and looked at the faces, "headed for the banks with 14 crew, one a friend of mine. She was a fine ship, Lunenburg built. The weather was settled. No fog."

"No fog in Fortune?" interrupted Sam, "The yarn is already unbelievable!"

"The Captain apparently put into St. Pierre," continued Skipper Jim, "he may have had some freight, or the boys were lookin' for beer and French ladies. A lad from Boxy told me that a friend of his was in a tavern in St. Pierre and saw a brawl between the b'ys off the *Blackduck* and a group of French trawlermen. Over some women it was. 'E said that a trawler took off just after the *Blackduck* next morning. Anyway, she left just after daylight, again settled weather," he paused, "She was never heard from again: the families, everyone, searched sea and shore—nothin'. No clue ever turned up. She just disappeared."

"Dat was '43 or '44 wasn't it? During the war. Me sons der were more scary t'ings below water than above it in dem days! We none of us knew what was goin' on around 'dese coasts," said the mate. "Dem German subs was everywhere—sure dey sunk ships tied up to the wharf in Bell Island!"

"If the Germans sank her, there might be information somewhere," said Matt, "They liked to keep records."

"Ders a song about the mystery of the *Blackduck,* I seem to recall."

They fell silent, listening to the low groaning of the ship and thinking of the hundreds of wrecks that had occurred along these wild coasts.

"We've had lots of sea mysteries," said Captain Windsor, "But this one is really strange as it's usually the weather that's the culprit … or, the ice," he added with a shrug. "You'll probably never get to the bottom of this one, Jim. How about a yarn with a happy ending next time?"

"When do you think we'll get out of the jam, Captain?"

"Maybe in a day or two. Wind's gone around to the southwest, which should loosen this stuff and move it off the coast. Then look to it boys, we'll have to be nimble and lucky or we could be sleeping on the white stuff, or worse."

The gale blew all night. The ship shuddered to the cacophony in the shrouds. The men on watch huddled in the lee and stared at ghostly shapes all around. Ice shifted and moaned like a giant monster rousing from hibernation. Before dawn, lantern light showed lanes of water forming and all hands manned the poles. Imperceptibly the darkness changed into a windy, white world and now lakes could be seen downwind. Ice pans grated the hull but suddenly there was open water toward the land. The *Winnifred Bea's* engine fired, and, after fifteen days of entrapment, twisting and turning, she escaped.

CHAPTER 23

▼

Labrador: Precambrian rock, moulded by glaciations, meets the western north Atlantic along a stately coastline of islands, tickles, fiords and bays into which pour rivers from countless lakes. Southern boreal forests change to northern tundra. Small Arctic-alpine flowers, dwarf birch and willows grow in a mattress of mosses and lichens. Caribou, bears, black and polar, seals, whales, salmon and cod all inhabit this duet of land and sea.

There are few places on planet earth that combine stark beauty with such a challenge to human habitation. Similar latitudes in Europe luxuriate in temperate climates. Here the polar current wraps a frigid arm around its treasures and points an arctic finger far south, bringing with it the beautiful terror of fog and ice and limiting summer to a few weeks. Matt recalled Sir Richard Grenfell's words on first seeing this coast in 1892: *'glorious sun on a blue sea, towering icebergs of fantastic shapes flashing all the colours of the rainbow, mist capped cliffs with feet bathed in dark rich green Atlantic water, edged by a line of white breakers—a very riot of magnificence.'*

In this setting, place the astounding adaptation of Eskimos, the stamina of roving Indian bands, the tenacity of missionaries and white settlers, the exploits of summer fishing fleets, and the valiant tableau of Labrador is complete.

Diary June 23rd, 1952

Sailed into Davis Inlet in early morning—about 20 tents under a hill at the head of the bay. Smoke rising straight up. Great excitement—first ship of the season. Captain anchored at mouth of bay and Naskapi Indians began unloading supplies.

Two Indian women paddled to the ship and took me up the inlet to the village. All the women, children and dogs were standing on the shore when we arrived. Much chatter and laughter, which peaked when I slipped climbing the steep bank, dropped my black bag, which was immediately urinated upon by a husky. That certainly broke the ice.

Conditions appalling; 10—15 people per tent plus 5—10 dogs. Stoves made from old gasoline cans were placed in the tent's center making it unbearably hot inside. Boughs on the floor, garbage, refuse, and among it all, babies and puppies. Babies and children malnourished, many with bronchitis and pneumonia—a complication of a recent measles epidemic that caused several deaths. Probable cases of tuberculosis. I took the infants outside in the fresh air and examined them on the clean moss. Gave penicillin injections. Gave instructions via Father Seguin, the R. C. Priest. Felt overwhelmed. Left vitamins. Many diagnoses. Two cases, almost certainly tubercular, must be transferred to St. Anthony. Discussed situation with the priest in the tiny new church just completed of rough spruce and balsam. The people, amazingly, seem happy and always ready to laugh.

The ladies paddled me back to the ship late in the day to delighted cheers from the shore. We leave tomorrow. Feeling inadequate. It's obvious I can only scratch the surface of this problem.

The next seven weeks were spent coasting between Hebron in the north and Hopedale in the south, where every two weeks, they met the *S. S. Kyle* with supplies from St. John's—always a festive occasion.

Then it was late August. Matt watched the first large snowflakes slowly fall, with the sombre Kaumajet Mountains for a background, and disappear into the dark sea. Was it a metaphor for life? He tried to define his mood; there was an element of euphoria in one who, with only academic attainment, found himself alone in a position of authority and responsibility. He remembered the looks of hope on the faces of the dying, as if he were the Saviour. The old Eskimo swollen with fluids backed up from a failing heart, who after digitalis and diuretics, lost 20 pounds and regained breath and thin ankles; the Eskimo women had their babies without calling him—he would hear this from the mission wife. But one day she rushed him to a tiny wooden shack, with stones on the roof to keep boards from blowing away, and filled with the detritus and smells of human-canine existence. There, on a low corner crate, lay an Eskimo, round and passive, who had been in labour for 36 hours with her 3rd pregnancy. What emotion was in those brown eyes that fixed on him? He could not be sure. He held her hand. He saw fatigue and eyes too dry for tears.

Breach presentation. With difficulty, he swept one leg down, then the other, and the baby entered this world feet first. The Eskimo features changed from exhaustion to joyous animation at the sound and touch of new life.

Tooth extractions, cuts, fractures, fishhooks, more tooth extractions.

He felt a feeling of euphoria mixed with respect for all the lives unfolding in the austere splendour of Labrador. Here were thousands of miles of awesome geology unfolding along a truculent coast, from the 3.8 billion years old granite-gneiss of the black Torngat Mountains southward to the sedimentary rocks of the Belle Isle Strait. Only mighty rivers subdued the mountains, flowing from headwaters at the height of land that was the border with Canada. All this was pummelled by the most boisterous weather available anywhere on the planet at these latitudes. However, there was also sadness and concern. He had met the Moravian missionaries, an Eastern European sect that had broken away from Catholicism 100 years before Martin

Luther. They had come to spread their version of the Christian gospel to Labrador as early as 1752 when John Christian Erhardt arrived in Nain with four missionaries. What zeal they had! What evangelical energy to convert the heathens! He wondered was the grief of death less intense for the Inuit after conversion than it was in the timeless isolation of their previous remarkable culture? Would God have sentenced them to eternal damnation for not knowing He existed? How could they have known? Did the Moravian efforts at conversion represent altruism, or was it arrogance? Well-intentioned evangelicals in a blanket of religion and homeopathy had nurtured this fragile society. There were problems, huge problems—the result of cultural collisions. European diseases ravaged the natives; the barter system, while preventing starvation, entrenched poverty and diminished initiative and respect. He thought of Thomas Grey's line, *'But knowledge to their eyes her ample page, rich with the spoils of time did ne'er unroll ...'*

He had grown. He had time to think and read. He was suddenly aware that answers depended on forming the right questions and this required intellectual freedom. Again, he exulted at his good fortune in having escaped the snares set for young intelligences by a species itself still ensnared in herd instincts. Science had wriggled loose from these bonds and was an amazingly successful formula; an individual human brain, forming hypotheses, submitting these to experiment and peer appraisal, could then in time, perhaps contribute to the true knowledge of the race. He said goodbye, shouldered his duffle bag and, with a last fond look at the *Winnifred Bea*, walked up the gangplank of the *S. S. Kyle* for the trip south to St. John's.

As the Kyle cleared the harbour, Matt looked back at the twilight mountains and thought of the lives unfolding on that stern shore; each an individual, adrift on the sea of fate, forever alone but always needing other beings; beings that were essential for early sustenance and later ego—each with their dreams and passions, their fears of being alone and of their ultimate fate: so few things controllable; so much random chance; only two certainties—life and death. Sentience adrift. No wonder the thirst for warmth, succour, companionship.

Maybe the missionaries supplied more than he realized. What had he done? He had changed a few lives, no doubt, but he was the real beneficiary. He had acquired a new understanding of the resilience and courage of life.

CHAPTER 24

▼

Heart's Content
Sept 10/53

Hello B'y,

Guess you be back docterin' by now—you're some smart to get an education. I tries to get me b'ys to school but they're crazy for fishin' b'y. Yes b'y—you never seen nothin' like it—crazy for troutin' and goin' in the woods and everyt'ing to do with water.

You should 'ave seen the whales in the harbour today, like crazy after the herrin'. Rearin' up and splashin' almost into the brook. Ole Josh Sinyard was watchin' and 'e says, "let me see one more 'ting as excitin' as dat and I'll leave this world wid no regrets."

B'y we put Jonathan to work for sure—good cod and lobster. E's gone back to school strong as an ox and wit a few dollars in 'is pocket.

Dere's a report out about da poor feller's arm you and Jonathan found. They say the bracelet had a swastika on it and a number 69—somet'ing and initials W.P. Says it was a German submariner most likely. Strange. Now b'y, last week da weather was quite civil so I says to Mike let's go and 'ave another look off Freshwater brook. Well, my son, you wouldn't believe how clear da water was—no current to stir t'ings up. Well, about a gunshot south of where you found the bones, only 100 feet offshore where it dropped off real sudden, sure there's a wreck. Yes b'y, sure as your born, with 'er bow stickin' up and the pilot house off to one side, and sea-

*weed clinging to everything. Lard Jasus, we was some excited!
I t'ought you'd like to know right away. The police are comin'
over wit a diver.*

*Must go pick a few berries. I'm cleanin' me old gun for the
partridge.*

Cheerio,

Tom

P.S. Nanny Regular came through her operation da best kind.

Matt smiled as he reread the letter. A month after Tom had writ-ten, the wreck had been identified—well, almost. The schooner's name had been lost but the homeport was Fortune and some gear, a toolbox, had been identified as belonging to Ezra Rowe, the mate. Everyone was convinced that the wreck was the *Blackduck.* However, the mystery only deepened. The story of the bones and then the find-ing of the wreck off Seal Cove had aroused great interest in Trinity South and indeed across the whole island. The locals scratched their heads, but could not recall the loss of a schooner in that area. Now it seemed it must be the wreck of the *Blackduck,* but that ship had dis-appeared off the south coast during the war and she was headed southeast for the Grand Banks. How could she have ended up in Trinity Bay hundreds of miles off course? Could the wreck be con-nected to the bones and the bracelet found nearby? The RCMP had the file and rumour was they were in touch with the West Germans.

Matt leaned back in his chair and gazed into the wood fire. When he had first read Tom's letter, he wondered where he had heard the name *Blackduck* before. Then suddenly he remembered. His mind went back to the fos'cle of the *Winnifred Bea,* trapped in Arctic ice off the Labrador coast. He remembered faces around the fos'cle table in the glow of kerosene lamps, each face a composite of its own anima-tion, the stamp of heredity and the entropic sculpting of time. Old Skipper Jim had taken a few puffs on his pipe and then told about the mystery of the schooner *Blackduck* out of Fortune, which had disappeared below the sea horizon in good weather, never to be seen again—until now—maybe. How indeed did she come to be wrecked off Heart's Content?

CHAPTER 25

▼

The class of '54 had graduated and dispersed like autumn leaves. Matt had decided to do post graduate studies in Internal Medicine and was now an assistant resident at the downtown metropolitan General.

It had been a long day. The hospital seemed to crowd in on him. "Somewhere," he thought, "waves are crashing on sea coasts, gulls hovering and sailboats heading to win'ard." Rounds with the chief, an emergency in I.C.U., and a case presentation with the interns at 11. He was working on a paper for publication, Pulmonary Hypertension, (high blood pressure in the lung circulation), and had reviewed drafts in the afternoon.

Feeling a little buoyed by a coffee, he went to make rounds on 2A, the medical ward. Mr. Graslyn had a recent myocardial infarction and the weakened left ventricle was letting fluid build up in the lungs. Matt watched the jugular column of blood slow dance, while he listened to the fine bubbles in the lungs and the muffled clapping of the heart valves. The aura of death was in the dark corners and on the shiny green walls of the room, where for three human beings, the final curtain was in various stages of descent.

Now aware of perfume, Matt looked up to see nurse McIntosh standing nearby. She was slim and dark, with long hair and a Celtic face. He had seen her before and it seemed they always had some medical item to discuss. She smiled. They discussed Mr. Graslyn's care and he wrote orders, feeling his fatigue lessen, forced out by some rising expectation.

It was the week before Christmas and the staff was decorating.

"Excuse me," she said in a low voice, "I'm decorating this window for Mr. Graslyn. Come and have a look before you leave."

Later he returned. She stood on the radiator painting Merry Christmas on the window. The last rays of a December sun, through a winter-brittle sky, shone through the glass and through her uniform, projecting a luminous image of statuesque anatomy. He stood a few feet away. Sensing his presence, she looked over her shoulder, turned again to the window, dipped her brush and just below Merry Christmas, printed Walnut 5-6804. They had not spoken a non-professional word, but the stage was set. The ancient ritual was unfolding. At 7:30, rejuvenated by anticipation, he dialled the number.

"Hello."

"I liked your window decorations."

"I'm so pleased."

"Are you alone?"

"Can you come over?"

"Yes," he answers.

"220 St. Andrews Street, Apartment 204. Ring and I'll let you in."

He showered in the euphoria of anticipation, ate a bit, signed out, bought a rose and grabbed a cab. Inside the foyer at 220 St. Andrews, he grinned at himself in a mirror, murmured, 'don't pinch yourself', and rang the bell.

The door of apartment 204 opened at the first knock. The room was lit only by city lights and a few candles. There was incense in the air and the low sounds of music. She was silken and soft. The world narrowed to one intense flame. A lifetime of constraints disappeared as reason fled before passion. Emboldened senses fanned the final fireworks in consciousness.

Her breathing was quiet now. He had been amazed by the intensity of her orgasm and the repetitive ongoing abandon of passion. It was 30 minutes before they spoke, lying in a cocoon of intimacy, then timelessness in warmth, wine and conversation. When they parted, responsibilities on 2A were only a few hours away.

Later he phoned and she told him she was to be married in 4 days. The currents of human behaviour, he thought, run murky and deep.

CHAPTER 26

▼

Flight 264, American Airlines, touched down at 5:32 p.m., as the western sky was surrendering colour to the tropic night—Lat. 13 05'N, Long. 59 35'W—Barbados. Jonathan had never been to the tropics, except in childhood imaginings fuelled by *Masterman Ready* and *Treasure Island.* His Uncle Jed had sailed salt cod from Newfoundland to the Caribbean, returning with a hold full of rum to foster dreams on cold nights, and had many yarns of high seas adventures during prohibition.

The sense of excitement and exoticism increased as he felt the warm soft air of the Islands and glimpsed tropical vegetation. His companion, Clayton Bonfield, moustached and crew cut, with a military bearing that belied his role as a physics professor, had lived near Bridgetown for a year after leaving Oxford.

Much had happened in the past three years. It had become apparent that Jonathan belonged to that small elite to whom mathematics was second nature. Fortunately and strangely, it appeared to onrushing science that Mother Nature's fundamental secrets could be written in mathematical symbols. Jonathan had excelled at his studies, doors opened easily and he had accepted an offer to study under Dr. Bonfield at the University of Southampton in England.

An hour later they were sitting on a bench in front of their cottage, sipping rum punch and watching white caps come roaring out of the sea darkness, only to end as suffix on the sounding sands. Distant piquant notes of a steel band rose and fell on the breeze.

"This meeting will be quite general," said Clayton. "They're a varied lot and that will dilute things considerably. What are you reading?"

"Fern Hill."

"Ah, our friend Dylan Thomas. Read me a verse please."

> *'Now as I was young and easy under the apple boughs,*
> *About the lilting house and happy as the grass was green,*
> *The night about the dingle starry,*
> *Time let me hail and climb*
> *Golden in the heydays of his eyes,*
> *And honoured among wagons I was the prince of the apple*
>   *towns*
> *And once below a time I lordly had the trees and leaves*
> *Trail with daisies and barley*
> *Down the rivers of the windfall night.'*

"Hmm. Poetry is a high attainment of consciousness," said the professor. "A distillation of word associations into image, simile and metaphor and nobody does that better than Thomas, a combination of alcohol and Welshness, I suspect."

"Maybe that's how we think," said Jonathan, "via word association retrieved from memory. Poetry may be close to our own thought and that's why it's a pleasurable challenge."

"Pleasurable indeed," said Clayton, "but I'm turning in. Seminar's at 9:00 a.m."

The next morning, with the sun already well above the palms, Jonathan made his way from the curving beach, past the pool, to a garden where chairs were arranged in a semi circle. Clayton Bonfield, still looking military despite a silk shirt, flowered shorts and sandals, was reading his notes. Jonathan took a chair half way back and watched as people arrived. At 9.05, Clayton walked to the front and looked over the chattering group.

"Good morning and welcome everyone. This will be an informal discussion lead by a few pathfinders. We anticipate input from all. The Topic is knowledge; sources and effects on human behaviour. I'm smiling now because I just heard Jeremy say 'Life is a relay race and the baton is DNA.'—just thought I'd pass that along." He shrugged and pronated his palms as a few groans ensued. "We want to focus on the nature of knowledge because what a society believes should determine its behaviour. Looking at history it would appear that much of our global family is misguided. Is there something wrong with the quality of knowledge?

"There is great irony in the present state of humanity. In the early days, in the Age of Reason in Western Europe, it seemed that the great harvest of scientific knowledge would remove superstition from human minds and, through education, bring on a golden age. However, the progress in science was so dramatic and immense that the vastness of the knowledge discovered became unmanageable. Science has fractured into many sub specialties, each becoming a separate discipline isolated by its own technical language. Science has difficulty communicating with itself, let alone with the citizenry. How sad. The great promise of knowledge is foiled and the confused citizen is prey, once again, to superstitions that continually spring up in great numbers. The world today is a terrifying example of what can happen when large groupings of humanity follow irrational creeds. But education remains the answer. We just have to find ways to communicate.

"Having achieved the ability to ponder and store experience, via human memory and libraries, we have the responsibility to ourselves and all biology to use this knowledge to decipher further mysteries of our Universe and, assessing the situation, to make decisions in the best interests of the present and future possessors of the genetic template.

"It is probable that the first topic listed—Religion vs. Science—is a spurious one in that there is no real relationship between the two. However, they both vie for the minds of man. Research vs. Revelation. I surrender the floor to Maureen Wilson, a post doc student in The Ancient Religions."

Maureen rose and nodded toward Clayton. She wore a snug green blouse, a beige mini skirt and green shoes. Her hair was pulled back in a ponytail that seemed to control a persistent smile.

"Thank you Clayton," she began, "That was an Anglo Saxon beginning on such a lovely morning—I want to laugh and sing—to praise somebody or something for the energy of the morning. Just look at the flowers, listen to the sounds!" She held up her hands and was quiet for seconds. "There, I rest my case." She began to walk away, then twirled and returned. "Just kidding! Now I am going to spoil everything by reading a paragraph I wrote last evening." She searched for her glasses.

"The urge to look beyond ourselves for answers has been a characteristic of all societies as far back as anthropology can reach. Brilliant minds have devoted their lives to the elaboration of concepts of deity. The application of such knowledge has inspired masses of humanity. How can we discard a moral/philosophical thrust that through the sweep of history, has encompassed the Tao of the Chinese, Buddhism and Hinduism on the Indian sub-continent, the Zoroastrianism of the Persians and the more recent flowerings of Judaism, Christianity and Islam? How can we dismiss the ecstasy, the assurance this knowledge of God has delivered to mankind struggling with his mortality? The totality of the involvement with a superior force is overwhelming. The great religions teach tolerance, altruism and humility. Then along comes science. The two sources should be complementary, not exclusive. One is a robust newcomer. The other a wisdom that goes back to the dawn of history. I have a foot in each. Maybe that's why the brain has two halves: one for facts, one for spiritualism." She took off her glasses.

"Indeed," said Justin Amorey, a colleague of Claytons who sat next to Maureen, "and there is scarcely an animal from The Egyptian Scarab to The Hindu Elephant that, at one time or another, sappy Homo sapiens has not bowed down to and worshipped as a God. Here is my opening paragraph.

"Let us begin to put things into perspective: We have a Universe—orbiting one of its billions of stars there is planet Earth on which Life has appeared. Of the many millions, nay billions, of species that have existed, only one, Homo sapiens, has the ability—at least to some extent—to understand himself and his Universe. Can you imagine what a hash we have made of this astonishing potential? Each human child is born untutored—a Tabula Rasa. How should we now proceed to write on this clean slate? Is it not unreasonable, nay criminal, to program this innocent with myth as opposed to reality, with religious fantasy as opposed to scientific truth? Has not programming with superstition contorted our past and bedevilled our present?" He sat down. The surf sounds seemed louder in the silence.

"Now here is our Philosopher—your turn Joseph," said Clayton.

A tall handsome Nigerian, Joseph Ayiede, stood and crossed his arms.

"Good morning Clayton and all. At least no one will accuse me of being an Anglo Saxon even if I am didactic in paradise." After scattered applause, he continued, "Philosophy has been part of both reason and revelation. It is all about thinking and therefore has been the fuel that has driven the renaissance in cognition over the last few thousand years. It tries to find an explanation—always the questions of why and how. The great religions all came up with similar answers that are authoritarian, undemocratic: giving answers that are not to be challenged. The Persians, Greeks and modern science accelerated an interest in understanding, in the explanation of our being. Modern Philosophy, bedazzled by its success, has begun to chase its tail into obfuscation; just a temporary state of affairs one hopes. Meanwhile, my colleague on my right has seized the initiative I feel. Jane Fetterley, please say a word on behalf of Psychology."

Jane looked small and demure in a long white dress.

"Our interest as psychologists is not as much who is right or wrong—reason or revelation—but what are the states of human cognition that lend themselves to certain beliefs and subsequent behaviour. The human brain is slow to mature in individuals and to adapt in cultures. Some evolutionary psychologists think this slow adaption was appropriate for hundreds of thousands of years around the caveman hunter/gatherer period because little changed. The startling onrush of change in the last two thousand years, especially in the last two hundred years, has left much of our thinking primitive and inappropriate. This, they believe, may account for the bizarre beliefs and behaviour afflicting modern day society. Our difficulty has been that the secrets of the human brain, read consciousness, have not been easily available to measurement. There is currently a strong trend in psychology toward scientific investigation of human behaviour, that is, behaviour explained by neurophysiology, which I find very exciting. Maybe we will explain both priests and scientists at the molecular level. That is all I will say for now."

"Thanks Jane. That brings us to Professor Wilkins and Physics."

Wilkins rose and nodded a bold white head.

"Priest is least and quest is best and never the twain shall meet." Groans. "Well now, the two entities have little in common except that they greatly affect many aspects of people's lives. We possess the wonder of the evolved brain. The scientific method has been amazingly successful in unlocking the secrets of the universe. That our brain, evolving from original energy, should seek to explain itself should be a source of scientific ecstasy—a state usually attributed to theologies. Both science and theology are important at this stage. One waxes, one wanes, one hopes! Dogma is dangerous. Theology should begin where science ends, so it will necessarily be a moving frontier; an explanation based on faith; an explanation of the diminishing void of the unknown."

"Discussion please."

Susan: "Why would an adherence to the two topics be combined in many individuals, religious scientists and scientific theologians?"

Andrew: "Religious belief is a powerful influence which is almost ineradicable when programmed from birth. Most scientists do not hold orthodox beliefs but some can fall back on the security blanket of childhood fantasy when faced with life's vicissitudes. Some also carelessly use reference to the supernatural as metaphor, which can confuse the real message."

Jonathan: "People should have easy access to scientific knowledge. It's essential for intellectual growth. The problem is not with religion, a separate entity really, but with science that divides itself into walled-off disciplines that develop their own language and impede dissemination. Is there some self-serving here? The lack of knowledge in the man on the street is quite astounding in this supposed information age."

The sun disappeared behind a cloud and gusts were busy in the palms. A short goateed man stood in the back row.

"How can we explain the fact that this special animal, to this day, has opted, in the great majority, to leave explanation to God."

"I would suggest," answered Justin, "that when our consciousness had evolved the capacity to love, to wonder and to fear, it was necessary to find an extirpation for the dreadful anxiety that can accompany those states. The God concept filled the bill—someone to succour us and even save us from oblivion—hey, heaven can wait but it sure sounds great! Our emotions ran ahead of our intellectual development and spawned God. Then human power brokers grabbed the concept and the amazingly powerful earthly religious regimes resulted. As a poet put it:

> *'An infection of humanity*
> *Captures and controls!*
> *Forms groups that hate,*
> *Then tribes and nations on each other prey—*
> *This anxious greedy vandal,*

Outsmarted by himself,
Befowls his nest
And blames himself on God'.

"Boy," Susan said, "that poet was in a bad mood!"

Andrew: "Science doesn't have a C.E.O. and marketing board like religion: everlasting bliss or everlasting pain. Take it or leave it!"

"Maybe science needs temples and music."

"Truth is the greatest temple."

"On that note," the chairman annouced, "time is up. At 9:00 a.m. tomorrow, we get down to specifics: *Quantum Theory* by Dr.Hoffman. See you then."

Jonathan and Professor Bonfield sat at a table on the beach. The fading light illuminated sailboats riding on the quiet swell. Tropic night enchanted with its warmth, starlight and the sound of surf. Jonathan sipped a scotch and thought of another Island besieged by Northern seas.

"I'd like to read you this by a Mr. F. Boas, written in 1913," said Clayton.

'*People think differently in different cultures not because they have different mental equipment but because all thought reflects the tradition to which it is heir, the society by which it is surrounded and the environment to which it is exposed.*'

"Well said. Self-evident maybe, but not really comprehended. The newborn may have a fixed genetic inheritance but is helpless to influence the circumstances of childhood, which will indeed determine how he thinks, who she is. Whoever gets there first has the greatest influence: religion, nationalism, local traditions. The die is cast before the brain can mature."

"To paraphrase Wordsworth, The child is father to the man is father to the child," said Clayton.

Jonathan sipped his drink before replying, "The belief in myth and mystery is so ubiquitous that this in itself is used as an argument for the occult. It appears that when our brain realized our vulnerability, anxiety began and the need for reassurance arose—hence the gods. I recall lines by R. A. Parsons:

> *'The river has the movement of a psalm*
> *And every woodland note without pretense*
> *Seems tuned to worship and to reverence;*
> *Then do I feel a sympathy abound*
> *With everything about my pathway round'.*

"That's striking."

"There is a lingering wish/fantasy to be comforted by some saviour".

"The critic called it, 'the characteristic response of the lyrical sensibility'."

"This penchant you mentioned makes us vulnerable indeed. The influence may come from sources that desire power as well as the stultifying effects of tradition and local culture."

"Only in the scientific method is there a built-in assurance, via peer review, that straying from the truth will not long go unrecognized," added Jonathan.

"Science is the gold standard. Myth and mysticism should have entertainment value, like Santa Clause," chuckled the Professor. "Oh well, let's enjoy the scene."

It was hot. Jonathan fell asleep on the balcony where the surf dominated the night sounds. Shortly after dawn, he was startled by a cry. "Help! Help!" A high-pitched, frantic request. He struggled into his trunks as the cries persisted and ran toward the beach, past signs that said, Danger-High Surf. A woman ran toward him.

"There's someone lost in the surf!"

A small group of people milled about at water's edge, pointing out to sea.

"What's the problem?"

"A woman went wading, got caught in the undertow", said a security guard. "Surf's too high. I wouldn't go in d'ere, mon."

Jonathan looked where the guard pointed. Nothing. Only swollen green waves that broke and crashed in fury on a coral outcrop about 75 yards to his left. Then, for a moment, a dark object, a head, rose on a wave and disappeared. He ran into the water, following the suction of a receding wave. The next breaker threw him tumbling back. He ran out again and grabbed a stake he had noticed on his right, and held on as the water hissed by. Then he pushed further out and dived into the next green wall just below the breaking top. He was submerged in sudden silence. He swam hard and surfaced beyond the surf line. He swam to get further out. Here the motion was a bumpy up and down. He swam in the direction of the girl. Had she gone under? No. There again was the head, now blond in the morning sun.

He stopped swimming about 15 feet away from the girl who was floating on her back. They were about 90 yards off a line of coral on which the surf was crashing with frightening violence. A few yards closer in and they would be in grave danger! As each wave crest passed, it felt like he was on a mountain of water about to be thrown into a valley of rocks. He swam within a few feet.

"My name is Jonathan," he called. "We are going to be all right! I want you to do as I say."

Her voice seemed calm and the words were partly lost in the sounds of wind and waves. "I panicked … but a transcendentalist … in a meditative state … I'm relaxed."

This seemed incredulous to Jonathan. What good luck. He was not a strong swimmer but the saltwater buoyancy gave him confidence. He swam closer, took a mouthful of water and dogged paddled, coughing.

"Great. I will catch you beneath the arms and we'll both swim on our backs."

Then the touch! Her skin was slippery firm. It was a moment of strange intimacy. They were together, alone, strangers in a wilderness of water, with injury or death a few yards away. She was above him, her head on his chest. "Now frog kick, frog kick! That's it." He drove hard with his legs. In his peripheral vision he now and then saw the foaming outcrop; the bearing wasn't changing. Were they caught in a current? A pang of fear arose, and then suddenly, he knew that they were moving.

"We're getting there. We're moving. Great. Another 50 yards and we can swim for shore. Slow, steady frog kicks—that's right."

One moment they were lost in a trough, the next floating high on a swell and could see the knot of people on the beach and hear encouraging cries. Now he knew they were well away from the coral reef.

"Okay," he said, "let's swim ashore. Hold on to me when we hit the breakers."

In a few moments, they were caught on a crest and tumbled swishing toward the shore in a welter of sand and foam. Many hands pulled them up the beach. She broke away from her friends and walked towards him, blood running down one shin, a determined, yet graceful stride, and an elegant face—wide set blue eyes above prominent maxillae. She reached out her hand.

"Thank you," she said in an English accent.

"You were brave," he said.

"No, I was foolish. The bravery is yours," and she was whisked away, down the beach.

Later, Professor Bonfield shook Jonathan's hand. "Rather a good effort before breakfast. What were you thinking out there?"

"Just wishing I was a better swimmer."

"Well, you rescued a beauty I hear. Let's get a coffee. We can still make the first lecture."

"I don't even know her name," said Jonathan. At that moment there was a shout from the beach.

"Hello Jonathan, mon!"

Jonathan picked up his morning coffee and walked out on the deck.

"Good morning."

"English to see you, Mon."

He followed the waiter through glorious foliage to the road. Five young people spilled out of an old taxi and there she was! They surrounded Jonathan and shook his hand. Two young men pummelled him on the back.

"My name is Vanessa," she said, "I'm so glad we found you. We are just rushing off to the airport. How can I thank you enough? Here is my address and phone number. May I have yours? Be sure to call if you are ever in England."

He wrote on an old envelope.

"Jonathan Shipman," she read, "Newfoundland … ah, oh dear, my geography! North isn't it?"

"Actually, south of London—it's the Mercator projection that distorts."

"How interesting. Sorry, but we must go. I'm sure we'll meet again."

They embraced.

"I'm so pleased you came by," said Jonathan.

Amid shouts of thanks, the taxi drove away.

Jonathan walked back with his empty cup—the coffee having spilled in the melee. "I didn't even tell her I'll be at Southampton University," he thought.

The card read:

> *Vanessa Walker*
> *Little Tythe House*
> *Top of the Wold, Near Winchcombe*
> *Gloscestershire,*
> *England*

Another dawn. Again, the steadfast tropic sun photon-kissed hibiscus and oleander. Jonathan walked barefoot at surf's edge and revelled in the morning. His sleep had been cluttered with dreams, or were they conscious wonderings, about the girl in the rip tide. By nine a.m., he was seated among chattering colleagues in the outdoor amphitheatre. The first speaker, a lanky boyish Dutchman, leaned on the lectern:

"Good morning ladies and gentlemen."

"The Universe and everything in it, including you and me—our bodies and sensibilities—consist of two things and two things only; Energy and Mass. And these two are readily convertible into each other so that a constant flux occurs, an interchange, accounting for all the incredible variety and evolution of our entire Universe. The study of this process is called Physics.

"Modern physics is like a three act play: Act I (1642). A child is born in a green and pleasant land between Nottingham Forest and the Holland of England. His discoveries—gravity, light and differential calculus—created classical or Newtonian physics that have provided a more or less common sense underpinning for science ever since.

"Act II (1879), at Ulm Germany, Albert Einstein would conceive the Special and General Theories of Relativity, the concept of space-time, a universal concept of gravity and the relationship of matter, energy and time as expressed in the elegant equation ($E = mc^2$). This is the physics of the very large, requiring conceptions not always germane to common sense.

"Act III (1858) Kiel Germany. Max Planck. He intuited the idea that energy was emitted in packets or quanta. This led quickly to the Bohr atom and the subsequent elaboration of the world of the very small; of atoms and subatomic particles that inhabit the complex, or astounding one could say, world of quantum mechanics. This physics frequently requires the suspension of disbelief.

"To quote Nadeau and Kofatos, 'Classical (Newtonian) physics is a workable approximation which seems precise only because the largeness of the speed of light and the smallness of the quantum of action, give rise to negligible effects.'"

Jonathan's mind wandered. The screen filled with graphs and numbers became liquid green, in which long blond hair washed to and fro festooning a blurred face: the incongruity of two strangers, suddenly dependent on each other. Now he knew who she was!

CHAPTER 27

▼

In Heart's Content the morning was misty and calm. Sam and Tom were hauling crab pots out in the bay and Roseanne had gone off somewhere. The kitchen clock chatted along to ten thirty. Rachel sat in front of her mirror. She felt an inner despair; there was so much to do. Things were slipping away from her. Tiredness. Lethargy. Arguments with Sam just seemed to happen. She had lost that feeling of wanting to be close to Sam, of intimacy. Sex was perfunctory and orgasm a memory. What was happening to them, to her? She looked at her reflection—lustreless eyes that seemed detached, sunken. She touched her hair and saw large fingers. Through the window, the misty sun wrapped the chestnut tree in a loveliness that was too much for her mood and she wept, wept for a long time, a convulsive frustration trying to find an exit. When she looked again in the mirror, she could see only one-half of her anguished face. Shocked she grabbed a book—only half the page was visible! Rachel closed her eyes. A jagged, golden saw interrupted the reddish retinal darkness! As she watched it became boomerang-shaped, moved to the perimeter of darkness and slowly disappeared. She opened her eyes; her mirrored face was intact but strange, coarse—even her teeth seemed different.

"What is happening to me?" Her grief suddenly flashed into anger. She struck out with her right hand sending perfume bottles flying. She grabbed one remaining bottle and threw it. The mirror shattered and a large shaft of glass fell, impaling her right forearm. Rachel felt a shiver of pain and watched a crimson flower unfold.

"Mom!" cried Roseanne, who had heard a crash as she opened the front door, "what happened?" She rushed upstairs.

CHAPTER 28

▼

It was late when Matt finished the office. He ate quickly at a Deli and returned to his apartment. He sat for a while sipping a scotch and recalling the day. He had been called from his lecture to the nurses to insert a temporary pacemaker in an old gentleman whose coronary artery disease had cut the 'wires' to his ventricles. He liked lecturing on the heart—a relatively simple organ, doggedly efficient and persevering, that had been raised to the metaphorical level of a major player in emotional consciousness by an enthralled public. In the mail was a letter postmarked, 'Heart's Content' and one from Darwin Biogenics Inc.

Feb. 2/62

Matt B'y,

Sure 'tis a good one we're havin' here now! You could smell it this mornin' when we got up. The glass was some low and still fallin', the sky bay gray and like it was crouchin' down. I says to Sarah, "B'y you're gonna see a lot of stuff flyin' around here today and none of it vertical. So now she's goin' full tilt from the N.E., the house is shakin', and the draft goin' up the chimney so hard the living room mat is 3 inches off the floor.

Was talkin' to Constable Grandy a few months ago. We were both huntin' down by Sooley's gullies. B'y he's got some nice dog, an Irish setter, but she's not trained yet, no sir! Still scratchin' 'is head 'e is over the Seal Cove mystery—said some nights 'e can't sleep t'inkin' about it! Says d'er are t'ree or four police forces workin' on it and 'e in the center! What a chance for fame! The poor guy is goin' nuts, what wit people tellin' 'im they saw dark shapes in the bay and heard gun fire an' all. The bones are from a young giant, 'e said. If t'was just a shipwreck, what 'appened to the crew? People could 'ave got ashore d'ere you'd t'ink. And the Swastika bracelet—likely a German from some war action—a body can float a long ways, I s'pose. Constable said d'ere could still be news from the Germans or the British.

Old Ray Burridge died last week. Some turn out at the funeral! Orangemen's band and the works. Yes b'y, he was goin' downhill for a good spell. Got forgetful. Two weeks before he died 'e put a shovel full of coal in Katie's stew. B'y she was some charged up!

Mom is doing really well. She's up and about and doing some light work. She takes lots of pills but it's only three weeks since the operation. Dad says Rachel is getting her soul back out of a bottle.

Anyway it's been a great winter. I hauled a lot of wood 'cross the mizzen pond. Found a great old cedar for a stem head and 'ad 'er sawed down the shore. Startin' to build an 18 footer next week we are.

Was out on the bay on Friday, just some slob ice. Shot a few turrs. Lots a seals b'y but dey're worth nothin' dem fellars up along wit' the Green Peace has got 'er all frigged up. You wouldn't want to be a codfish out d'ere now I can tell ya.

Me b'ys are still goin' to school but dey're lookin' over d'ere shoulders at everyt'ing except books.

Dat's great about Jonathan in England and look at you sure!

Take care, yes b'y

Tom

P.S. Sid Martin went to hospital last week wit' the kidney stones. Said he felt like he was pissin' a conner tail first. Said to say hello.

CHAPTER 29

▼

The green door opened and Rachel was wheeled into a room filled with white-coated individuals. The chatter quieted for a moment and then returned to previous levels. "Penguins," she thought, suppressing a chuckle, "a new large species of white penguins!"

"Your attention please," said a middle-aged man standing before a blackboard. He had heavy sideburns that connected with a black beard and seemed to hold up his jaw. He pushed a button and a white screen descended.

"Ladies and Gentlemen, the patient we are presenting today is Mrs. Rachel Shipman. We are an inquisitive but friendly lot, Mrs. Shipman, so do not be alarmed. My resident has already presented your story to the medical students. I turn the proceedings over to him."

"You've heard the history," said the Resident, a balding fellow, round and with a slight hesitancy of speech, "Mrs. Shipman won't mind if you ask questions and examine her, will you dear?" Silence. He ran his finger down a list of names. "Ms. Sibley, would you lead off please?"

Sonja Sibley's face reddened to the roots of her dark hair. She stood and walked over to Rachel, who was trying to keep her blue Johnny-coat from slipping off her shoulders. Sonja retied the top string and her tension eased. "When did you first see your family Doctor and why?"

Rachel told her story ending with "Well I went from bad to worse until I finally saw the gland doctor—Dr. Baggs was his name—and he told me I had—oh shh! I'm not supposed to tell!"

Sonja examined Rachel and then asked for the investigation results.

"Hold a moment," said the Resident, "please outline how you would investigate this case."

Sonja wrote a plan of lab tests and imaging on the blackboard. The audience now questioned Rachel and there was much discussion.

"How long were you in the Psychiatric Hospital?"

"For about two weeks after I cut myself."

"Were you on medication there?"

"Yes, I took those pills for about two months. They made me feel weird but relaxed. They were treating me for depression."

Dr. King, an Internist, flashed a slide on the screen showing Rachel's lab results.

By now Rachel was enjoying herself. All these earnest learned people, from youth to seniors, wondering and concerned about her!

"Alright Ms. Selwyn, what other tests would you like, and then please make a diagnosis for us."

"I would like to see a skull x-ray and a growth hormone level."

A skull x-ray flashed on the screen.

"The Radiologist says the sella turcica is enlarged. Growth hormone levels are consistently elevated."

"Well done Selwyn. So your diagnosis is?"

"Acromegaly" said Sonja, "but I must admit it only hit me when I heard someone mention it, then everything fell into place."

"Well done" said Dr. King, "Don't be too modest. The Resident will now give a summary of this disease."

Rachel listened. How amazing. A tiny tumour in her pituitary gland—the gland that hangs like a blueberry on a stalk from the underside of the brain and produces seven hormones controlling the entire orchestra of life—form and feelings. In her case, the growth hormone had been in excess and had made her bones thicken and deform.

"My word," thought Rachel, "if that little bit did so much, what about the rest of the brain and all the other organs? Our bodies are like a foreign language and the likes of us only know a few words. How can we know so little about ourselves? I guess we only need to know enough to have children—don't need to know much to accomplish that—and then work to put bread on the table. And there are the smart ones who tell you what to do, people in power like priests and dictators. They direct you along the same paths generation after generation—because we be dumb! But these doctors had escaped mostly hadn't they? Education—education was the answer! Had Matt and Jonathan escaped? But the powerful people tried to control education too. Was it too late for her to escape?" She lay back, relaxed, smiling at her new secret defiance.

CHAPTER 30

▼

Matt was sitting on the foredeck of the 40-foot Westerly cutter *Enchantress*, cocooned in the sounds and movement of the harbour scene. He leaned back against the sloping doghouse with his feet on the windlass as he spliced a noose in a shoreline. Gulls' cries and tinkle of halyards against masts came on the southwest breeze. Two berths away a lovely wooden sloop tugged against her lines like a ballerina waiting to burst on stage. The marina looked out on Southampton water that led south to the Solent, famed in story and one of the planet's centers of man's love affair with the sea. How amazing that he was here, he thought. Jonathan had called Matt in mid-winter from Southampton. Vanessa's brother, Nigel, needed crew to sail his boat to the Mediterranean next summer. Could he get away? They could cruise under sail and perhaps get started writing the book they had long discussed. It was very exciting. As luck would have it, Matt was considering a career change, a research position with Darwin Biogenetics, and had arranged to join the company in late autumn. It was also arranged that he would visit the parent company in England and facilities in Italy and Turkey during the summer. So here he was. He was bemused and warmed by memories of last week. He had walked along an English lane, through sunshine and tree shade, where hedges framed the green symmetry of hills rolling in sheep-flecked, mammary roundness to the horizon.

"Turn left at the top of the wold," she had instructed, "cross the cattle grill and you will see a slate roof above a cedar hedge." As he approached, he heard laughter and the gentle pop of tennis balls above the background of bees and wind rustle. A young woman and a boy were playing on a grass court, the scene made abstract by sunlight dappling through a spreading copper beech. She was tall and tousled in tennis whites, blond hair flirting with the light. Matt noted sun shadow on long thighs showing the ripple of quadriceps and hamstrings.

Vanessa, turning for a backhand, noted the stranger. She said something to the boy, and brushing her hair back, walked his way. He recalled her slim waist and an enticing pectoral symmetry. They had tea and chatted easily like old friends. He had a strange feeling that everything had changed. "Jonathan had rescued this beauty," he thought incredulously, "never did the sea surrender such pulchritude." She talked about university. She was having difficulty with Jean Paul Sartre, loving Dylan Thomas.

"Have you read Voltaire?" she asked.

"Not really," said Matt, his brain racing to recall. "Didn't they write on his funeral car the words: 'He gave the human mind a great impetus; he prepared us for freedom'."

"He's wonderfully exciting to read," said Vanessa, smoothing down her tennis skirt, "they say he was the most brilliant mind of the greatest century—the 18th, and his play Candide, one of the greatest of all time."

"I tend to put him in the same category as Bernard Shaw," said Matt.

They talked in the growing web of new acquaintance and the cocooning warmth, sounds and perfumes of an English summer garden. After her rescue by Jonathan, she had found Newfoundland on the map and was curious about Matt's life on the Island. Then, all too soon, an old land rover rolled over the cattle grill bringing Jonathan and her brother, Nigel. He had the urge to embrace her later as they left for the boat, but they shook hands and her last words were a source of hope.

"Have a safe voyage and we'll meet in Majorca."

CHAPTER 31

▼

Enchantress, under full sail, traced her wake on a robust sea. Alive, she trembled in the troughs, as close hauled, they slid southward with Spain's Cape Finisterre to port. Nigel joined Jonathan and Matt in the cockpit, where sheltered by lee cloths, they were warm in the westering sun.

"How's she going?"

"Being pushed a little to the west," replied helmsman Jonathan, "sails best at 40° to the wind on a heading of 192°, averaging around 6 knots."

"Just heard the weather from the BBC Shipping Forecast," said Nigel, "Gale in the Azores, force 9, may affect the Portuguese coast by early morning. Just as well we have lots of sea room. I'll get a fix and then let's have tea."

Later, sitting in the cockpit amid the hiss of passing seas and low music from the shrouds, they watched the sun approach the western horizon.

"So what are your highpoints so far … pretty friendly seas for a pair of Newfoundlanders, I expect?" asked Nigel.

"Hey, it's been great. My biggest shock to date was the height of the rocks in the channel after the tide ran out of Lezardrieux, to think we had sailed blithely through these waters a few hours before! Rounding the Raz de Seine in that thunderstorm was an eye-opener also. I don't think we have anywhere quite that devilish back home—such a witches' brew of rocks and boiling current mixed with fog."

"The smell of coffee and barbecued chicken in La Coruna after crossing the Bay of Biscay wasn't hard to take."

"Hey Matt, what about you? It seems to me Matt has been a bit pensive since he met your sister," said Jonathan, winking at Nigel. "He didn't pay enough attention to the Spanish girls and seems in a rush to get to Majorca."

"We'll put him in irons when we reach Majorca," said Nigel. "I'll take no chance with having colonial genes in this family."

Matt felt an inner serenity from pleasurable anticipation and the memory of English beauty, but he disguised it with, "If I have to eat your cooking for the next two weeks, irons won't be necessary. I'll be in sick bay."

The wind had dropped and the yacht moved at three knots through a listless sea.

A marvellous panorama unfolded in the West. The sea spread out before them reflecting luminous greens and blues until it merged with sunset vermilion. Higher in the sky, the soft blue of summer was dabbed with sunset clouds. Northward rose a panoply of cumulus, whose startling darkness seemed a malevolent presence in the riotous beauty of day's end.

Jonathan took the wheel. Matt and Nigel put a double reef in the mainsail and set a working jib in place of the genoa, then took to their bunks fully clothed with foul weather gear at hand, in anticipation of the storm.

Jonathan watched the light fade and the stars appear. Soon the wake was faintly aglow with the phosphorescence of disturbed minute life. The wind was fretful and moist just before mist. He thought of motion: forward, up and down and rolling in *Enchantress*; imperceptible rising and falling on the moon-pulled tide; the planet, whirling and swinging around the sun; the solar system rotating in an arm of its vast spiral galaxy; clusters of galaxies and superclusters all on the move; and inside him the torrential motion of blood, the molecular dance of biochemistry and the quantum energy flux in his brain that gave the glow of awareness. How wonderful this awareness.

The show began with flashes on the horizon—approaching and more vivid—now accompanied by the low rumble of thunder. The stars disappeared. All was blackness. Then the gale hit like an invisible fist. *Enchantress* shrieked and swirled like a wounded animal. Her port scuppers went under. Jonathan was thrown to leeward. His hands caught the port safety lines for a moment, but a hard, heaping sea tore him away and he submerged in the liquid tumult. Bruised and shaken, Nigel and Matt tumbled into the empty cockpit and saw Jonathan's safety line straining over the stern.

As good luck would have it, in those few moments, the mainsail had thrust *Enchantress* into the wind, the jib was backed, and amazingly the little ship was hove-to and riding the seas with a modicum of dignity.

Jonathan was hauled alongside and pulled aboard with a great struggle. The three exhausted men lay in a tangle on the cockpit seats, as *Enchantress* sailed slowly onward. Then Jonathan was bent face down over the mainsail slide where he had paroxysms of coughing and vomited seawater. Nigel secured the rudder amidships and was content to leave *Enchantress* hove-to.

In about an hour, the wind abated somewhat and they helped Jonathan down below to his bunk in the V berth. Matt ascertained there was good air entry into both lungs and that Jonathan had a cracked rib.

They released the jib and *Enchantress* ran away with the wind on her quarter.

At the wheel, Nigel could feel the testing of *Enchantress*. He controlled the pivotal rudder force that altered the balance between the thrust of water on the keel and the force of wind on sail. The exoticism of wild force was exhilarating.

For five hours, they drove westward, quartering the southeast gale, the situation boisterous but controlled. They sipped thermos tea and munched on hard biscuits from home. Then the gale passed on, leaving only lumpy seas, fatigue and shards of fog in the grey dawn. *Enchantress* resumed her course, parallel to the linear Portuguese coast, heading for Cabo St Vincente and the Strait of Gibraltar.

*   *   *   *

Enchantress lay stern-to on the Grand Paseo in Palma, Majorca. The mooring was crowded with old boats and new, many with seaweed hanging from the mooring lines that had not been hauled for months. The sounds of the city and harbour rose and fell on a brisk southerly breeze. The past ten days had been magic indeed—a sumptuous serving of history and geography, of exploration and the clash of Empires, all sensed from the deck of *Enchantress* sailing under ideal conditions through these storied waters—Cabo St Vincente and the 90° turn eastwards. To port lay Sagnes and the school of Henry the Navigator. To port again, the site of the Battle of Trafalgar where the white ensign had secured control of the planet's seas for 100 years by downing the Tricolour in fire and blood. Matt read Browning's 'Home Thoughts from Abroad ... *sunset reeking into Cadiz Bay ... Jove's planet rising silent over Africa ... In the farthest north east distance dawned Gibraltar, grand and grey.'*

Enchantress had docked at Gibraltar near the airport reclaimed from the sea. They provisioned and then roamed the ancient streets of this exotic focus of Empire. Spanish border guards were disgruntled as they traveled to the Moorish palace, the Alhambra, to experience the beauty of architecture and design, of water, light and foliage, below the snow-capped Sierra Nevadas. Then, one gray dawn, they shipped the lines and stood off northeast for Palma, where Vanessa would arrive in a few days and where they hoped to get more information about the bracelet on the skeletal arm that showed a swastika and the inscription U694 WP.

Matt sat across the cockpit table from Vanessa, aware of her nearness and watching her pin back long blonde hair in a ponytail. Jonathan's mind flashed her in green lumpy seas with tresses trailing like a jellyfish. From the galley came the aroma of bacon and eggs and then Nigel, wiping his brow and proffering a large frying pan filled with British breakfast. Plates were held out like the rounded mouths of hungry birds. They sat eating in angled sunshine that cast a truncated shadow of *Enchantress* on the trembling water.

"Right," said Nigel, scraping scraps to the mullet, "I'm rather confused about the mystery of the bones as I'm sure Vanessa must be. Would one of you please brief us in detail?"

"Okay," said Jonathan, pouring himself more tea and leaning back against the safety lines, "you start Matt."

"Sure. Well it's been almost ten years since we found the bones in the sand, part of the skeleton of a very large man. On the wrist was a bracelet, which, after cleanup, showed U694 on one side and W.P. on the other. Then a few weeks later, Jonathan's brother Tom, searching the area for the police, found a wreck about eighty yards from the bone site, in shallow water, which turned out to be the schooner *Blackduck*. Now the disappearance of the *Blackduck* was vintage folklore in Newfoundland because she vanished in good weather with no trace in 1942. I first heard the story when I was down on The Labrador."

"Then years later," said Jonathan, "The R.C.M.P. has obtained information from German authorities, only recently released, showing that there was indeed a German submarine U694 that operated in the Western North Atlantic in 1942 on a special mission. Also, the torpedo officer on board was one Wilhelm Prostner. That sub, however, was not lost in 1942. She was refitted in Kiel in 1943 and then sunk with all hands off Cabo Finisterre in early '45. Strange! Prostner was not on board when she was lost. German authorities have located a friend of Prostner who said she saw Wilhelm last in 1948. The friend thought Prostner had moved to Greece. She also said that Prostner had a cousin living in the village of Valldemossa on Majorca."

"So the plot thickens," said Nigel. "The arm didn't belong to Wilhelm Prostner, so what did the W.P. stand for? It seems like a long shot but I guess somebody should go to that address in Valldemossa and check out the cousin of W.P."

"Indeed," said Jonathan, "we have a day's work to do on the engine. Nigel and I are the most talented in that department. I suggest that Vanessa and Matt go up-country and sort this out."

"Good idea," said Nigel, "and Vanessa speaks fluent Spanish. We'll give you 36 hours to do the job."

Three hours later, they stood on the seawall, packing the rental car.

"We'll be back in 24 hours and really pitch in," said Vanessa. "I'm looking forward to visiting the Chopin Sands house en route."

"It's nice to see two people so interested in music," chuckled Nigel as the car drove away. "Hey, Jonathan, you pulled my lovely sister from the sea but she seems to be sweet on your friend."

"Great stuff. They seem well suited. Something may come of this."

"Emotions rule the day," mused Nigel, "intellect need not apply."

The morning was warm and humid when they left. 'Caplin weather' thought Matt, remembering the foggy, still days of early July, when the little fish stranded themselves in a strange sexual ritual on the pebble beaches of Trinity Bay.

They drove northward through river valleys, past olive groves and flocks of tinkling sheep. Flowers adorned trees and meadows. Craggy mountains, the children of fretful volcanoes, rose inland and ran in tumult to the North coast. They sipped coffee amid hibiscus and oleander, adrift in an intense state of awareness and anticipation, each glance and movement a part of the invitation.

Just before noon, they drove into the dusty Town of Valldemossa, nestled on the slopes of a four thousand foot mountain. the main street was stark in the light and eucalyptus shadows of a hot Spanish day. Stepping over a sleeping dog, they entered La Officina de Correos.

"Habla Inglesa, senor?"

"Un poco."

"We wish to contact a German gentleman who we are told lives in this village. His initials are W.P. He may be able to help us with a family matter."

The Postmaster looked annoyed and held the paper Matt had given him close to his glasses. "Needs a new prescription," whispered Vanessa.

"Manuel!" yelled the old man and a supple youth appeared from a back room. They gesticulated and talked rapidly and then the old man brushed by into the street. There he pointed to a hill on the north end of town and made a circular motion with his forefinger.

"El Pajaro Carnetera," he said, "about two kilometres. Ask someone there."

"Gracias," said Vanessa. The old man returned a faint smile, relieved that the intrusion into his afternoon was over.

Ten minutes later, they were walking along a curving road on the outskirts of town looking for number 36. "That's it," said Vanessa, pointing to a stone cottage set back 40 feet from the road. The scene was a riot of Nature's reclamation: chipped stones, straggling vines and one gnarled olive tree looking like some leftover from a petrified forest. They knocked, then pushed open a creaking door and looked inside.

The room was musty and unkempt but a kettle on the stove and kitchen utensils suggested recent occupation. Startled by a cackle, they turned to see an old woman covered in black and bending over a crooked walking stick. She gave a toothless grin and, beckoning with a bony hand, limped away, then turned and beckoned again.

Matt and Vanessa looked at each other, shrugged and followed.

The old crone hobbled horribly around a corner and another cottage came into view.

A dark haired woman, in a flowered dress, sat on the veranda holding a baby. They approached behind the old woman, who sat down on the doorstep and cried out, "Maria, Maria, Maria."

Vanessa spoke to Maria in Spanish. Handshakes, baby holding and conversation followed with much hand waving and pointing, and the next thing Matt knew,Maria was laying out bread, cheese and olives. After they had eaten, Maria took them back to the deserted cottage. In a cobwebbed corner, Matt found a box of books—Nietzsche, Goethe and other authors he did not recognize.

"Look at this!" exclaimed Matt. He had opened the cover of a dusty mahogany box. "It's a sextant—a lovely German sextant! I'm going to take it. Someone will steal it if we leave it here."

"No you are not."

"It's beautiful! It'll be destroyed."

"And the Guardia Civil will put you in jail and throw away the key if they catch you."

"Well I planned on sending it back to the owner," said Matt, reluctantly putting the box back where he had found it.

"Maria says two Germans lived here," said Vanessa, "they had many books and much music. I can't wait to tell you the details."

Inside a bedroom drawer, Matt found a newspaper picture of a man in uniform, his features not discernable. There was a seven-digit number written below. In another drawer was a wrinkled chart of the North Atlantic.

Later, after goodbyes and followed to the curb by the old woman, they walked back to the car.

"Here's the gist," said Vanessa, "Two Germans, brothers or cousins Maria thinks, lived there for about 6 years. Then they suddenly departed three months ago. Shortly afterwards two men, German police Maria says, arrived but nobody told them anything. I thought that was all but Maria, who cleaned for them sometimes, gave me this piece of paper with a phone number where she thinks they can be reached. It's a Greek number!"

They looked at each other and touched hands. The trail was still warm.

Later, in a setting of wild mountains and Spanish gardens, they visited the old Carthusian Monastery where Frederic Chopin and the authoress George Sands (Aurore Dudevant), had a winter affair. Here

Polish genius flowered, but passionate love was tamed by tuberculosis and a Mediterranean winter.

The grand piano looked pristine and seemed to smirk with memory. Pictures captured lifeless moments in time, all cold embers of the fires of passion and creativity that had added so much to the human acoustic dimension. As they left, with a tape of the preludes, Matt noted high cloud partially obscuring the moon.

They sipped sherry in a little cabana, apart from the main Inn. Subdued moonlight softened the trees and fell lightly on the distant sea. They washed their bodies in foaming warmth and lay together.

In the silence—a sound, distant, faint, rumbling—now gone. There it was again. Growing. Now a low, long pulsating wail. A growing rumble, closer, the long cry again and the panting of steam, now a roaring filling the room with rising sound, suddenly transformed to a decrescendo moan that sobbed away into the muffle of distance. They revelled in the warm symmetry of flesh, the epiphany of merging.

The Storm hit just before dawn. A long, low note of wind rushed up the ravine from the sea. Now the rumbling moan of thunder and the mounting gale—lightning flashes revealed the land in a cadaveric pallor—the house and trees besieged.

A few hours later, Aeolus had gone back to sleep. A sun-filled dawn showed the results of his tantrum: strewn trees, scattered tiles and sheds. They prepared to return to *Enchantress* but it was midday before the road was cleared.

Down the mountain road, they drove toward Palma on the southern shore. Everywhere was strewn debris from the unruly night. Now they were in the streets of the ancient city—its character moulded by numerous invaders from the earliest Phoenicians to the present-day tourists from Manchester.

The Guardia blocked their access to the Grand Paseo. Having parked the car, they walked around a corner onto the sea wall and were transfixed. The boulevard was scattered with wrecks of yachts, crushed hulls and broken spars. People were wandering in a state of disbelief. Just off the seawall, in a calm harbour, masts and hulls protruded in grotesque surrender above the water. Appalled, they rushed past the wrecks and suddenly there was *Enchantress*, lying on her starboard side, a ripped red ensign still jauntily hanging off the taffrail, and Jonathan sitting on the coach-roof, sipping a beer, his head wrapped in a large bandage.

"Be the Lard Jasus, b'y," said Matt, lapsing into his native dialect, "Looks like you've 'ad quite a shindig. Are you alright? Where's Nigel?"

"Me son, you missed it. She came blowin' like the bejasus from the south'ard. You never saw such a breeze. Dropped us all on the road like pickup sticks. Nigel's in the hospital but he's ok—broken ankle and ribs."

When they walked into Nigel's room, he was on the phone to his insurance company. His chest was bandaged and his forehead stitched. Vanessa kissed him. He and Matt touched hands.

"Sure glad you two weren't here. With four people aboard someone could have been killed. How was it on the mountains? Nurse told me they recorded winds of 100 mph up there."

"Well, ah, we heard some heavy winds and the Inn shook."

"And the roads were blocked by fallen tree," added Vanessa.

"And I expect the earth moved as well," thought Nigel. Then aloud, "Well, it was amazing. I had just turned in. Jonathan heard the sound and was looking at the wind gauge. "Nigel," he says. "It's 30 knots ... 40 ... Lord Jesus, it's 50 knots. Hit the deck!" Before I could get up the companionway, there was a crash and she shuddered. When I looked around, I couldn't believe my eyes. A huge wave was breaking over the boat. Then it sort of withdrew and the yacht hit bottom. The next wave picked everyone up and we went flying over the seawall. I saw Jonathan disappear in the foam. Several boats washed back into the harbour and sank."

For the next few days, Vanessa stayed in a three star pension nearby. Nigel hatched a plan to get the insurance money and use some of it to buy *Enchantress* back at a wreck price. He was already planning to repair her at a nearby shipyard. Vanessa and Matt told of the information from Maria and showed the slip of paper bearing the number Navpaktos 1673 8492. It was decided that Matt should make the call.

The phone rang five times, then a guttural, "Ja, Sigfried."

"Is Wilhelm there, please?"

"No. Who's calling?"

"Someone who knows of him, who wants to be a friend from the past."

"He's not here. He's crazy, said he wanted to see the Northern Ocean again."

"When did he leave?"

"Long time. Only had one postcard from Ireland, I think it was. You English?"

"No, Newfoundlander, ah, Canadian."

"He talked of Canada. Some frozen port. He's crazy."

"Was he a sailor, in the navy?"

A pause … "I talk too much. He's an old man. Let him alone."

Click.

Matt dialled the number several times, but there was no answer.

Matt crossed the street to a sidewalk café where Nigel, Jonathan and Vanessa were having coffee while watching the seaport scene; boats, old men and nets, cats and women in black. He related the phone conversation exactly while Vanessa wrote it down.

"Interesting," said Jonathan, "at least it appears there really is a Wilhelm Prostner who lived in Majorca as rumour had it."

Nigel lifted his foot off the sawdust-covered floor and placed the cast on a bench. "It really is thin gruel," he said, "You have bones, bracelet and the initials WP which can't stand for Wilhelm Prostner because he isn't dead. You've found him, most likely."

They were quiet for a moment.

"This mystery gnaws at me … I guess it's all a bit irrational, but Wilhelm's cousin sounded really defensive."

"So he wants to sail in a northern sea, probably Ireland, and that bit about a frozen part of Canada …"

"We'll have to report this to the police."

"What a good excuse to spend a few days in Ireland, looking for a Mr. W. P.," said Vanessa.

They watched a lovely ketch motor into the marina.

"Hey," said Nigel, "I'll have *Enchantress* shipshape in a year at the most. Some year soon, I want to sail her to your country and, if Matt hasn't lured my sister there before, I'll bring her along. Let's drink to the Voyage of *Enchantress*! To-morrow it's back to reality for us all."

A wild late summer storm had ended the voyage of *Enchantress*. The summer had been a poem of living seas, new landfalls, cultures and the sweep of history; ending on the exclamation mark of near disaster. Matt and Vanessa had fallen in love; their senses finely tuned to tingling optimism and anticipation, hearing an emotional symphony that easily drowned out the pedantic low chords of reason. Two years later, after Vanessa's graduation, Matt retraced his first walk up the wold and they were married overlooking a valley in 'England's green and pleasant land'.

Jonathan returned to studies in Southampton where he was studying hydrogen fuel cell technology.

CHAPTER 32

▼

Sam made up his mind to go sealing again with Skipper Tim Burnell. Swilin' they called it.

"You're too old for that, you foolish old coot!" said Rachel.

"Dad, it's not worth it," said Tom, "you'll only get pennies a pelt!"

"Skipper says the price will firm up to three dollars or more. Anyway it's not just the money—I got it in me mind to do it just one more time."

They left port early morning on March twentieth. The *Mary Anne* was a thirty-eight foot schooner, twenty years old. She had a ten-horse power Coker gasoline engine installed just a year ago—the first one along the whole coast. She chugged past Light House Point and then they set the sails. Passing Baccalieu Island by sunset, they could see the line of the ice 'front' gleaming on the horizon; ice that had formed in the ferocious cold of the High Arctic and drifted at a stately pace southwards on the Arctic current; ice floes that had collided one with another with colossal force that reared up a chaos of ice angles and forms; ice that would be the birthing platforms for a million seals; ice that now reflected the lowering light of a March day into the excited eyes of intrepid hunters; ice that, along with its abettors wind and sea, had killed hundreds of their countrymen.

For the next two days, they had light winds and good luck, with scores of pelts aboard.

Rachel was awakened early morning on March 23rd by gusts that shook the house. Outside was roaring darkness, and her oil lamp showed snow ghosts flitting by the window. The nagging concern since Sam left, erupted into sickening alarm as she pictured the little boat in winter seas. She warmed some old tea on the kitchen stove and sat in the rocking chair listening to the night; the chair before the warm stove where she had rocked the children when they had toothaches and fevers in the night; it was a secure and comfortable place of refuge. But the gusts and creaking were unbearable; she was beside herself with anxiety and could not stand the loneliness.

Tom had married Sarah last summer and had bought a house just a few yards away. She dressed quickly and fought the blizzard to his door, arriving snowy and breathless. Tom, awakened by the sound of the kitchen door, appeared besotted with sleep. They hugged in helpless alarm as the storm ripped up the night.

The next few days were a nightmare of fading hopes; the vicious storm had wrecked two vessels in Bonavista Bay but without loss of life. The Radio broadcast the news of the missing schooner and searching began along the Bonavista, Trinity and Conception Bay coasts with no sign of the Mary Anne. Jonathan and Roseanne came home and the family shared its grief with the community.

April arrived with strong easterlies. Arctic ice filled the bays and increased the damp chill of early spring. Hope had vanished. The children departed leaving Rachel alone, coping with everyday things and a desolation all her own.

Some three months later, on a quiet summer morning in July, hunters rowed their dory to a small island about a mile offshore. After landing on a tiny pebble beach, they climbed fifty feet to the rocky summit. There, eastwards down the sloping crags; they saw a mast and the scattered wreckage of a boat. They approached with trepidation. The vessel was crushed and shorn as by a great fist. On the shattered bow was the name *Mary Anne*.

They gathered a few items—a black kettle, parts of a rifle and a torn jersey.

One of the men worked his way along the shore. A few yards to the west, he pulled himself over a turfy outcrop with the sea teasing twenty feet below. To his left was an opening in the rocks partially covered with blackberry moss making a cave-like entrance. Peering inside he was horrified to see two skeletal faces leering in death towards him and the light.

The day Sam was buried preened in stark contrast to that frightful night when cold snuffed out the fire in his heart. Birdsong at dawn found wild roses on the hills and irises rooted in wetlands, the land and sea held hands and a warm breeze bore traces of the Great Continent to the west.

> *Oh hear us when we cry to thee*
> *For those in peril on the sea!*

The sounds of ritual were lost in the surrounding woods. Back in the house with the closed blinds, the Minister loosened his collar and conversation and even humour fought against the sense of loss; against the sea-god who gave but seemed to demand the regular sacrifice of those who dared to live and work on the fringes of his domain.

For Tom and Jonathan it meant sorrow—sorrow at seeing Sam's boat riding alone on her collar, and memories prompted by nature's signposts; the first loquacious flight of geese, the tug of squid, the whirr of the ptarmigan—signposts they had observed together down the years.

For Rachel it was being alone in the long nights.

CHAPTER 33

▼

The *Cormorant*, a thirty-six foot ketch, slipped away under sail from her sheltered berth in Valencia, on the southern tip of The Irish Republic. Some hang-a-shores of recent acquaintance threw his lines and shouted farewells as Wilhelm Prostner steered his little ship toward the open sea. A few hours later, the green hills were fading low astern and she was standing, close hauled, to the northwest. He felt a euphoria born of excitement and anticipation that he had not experienced for a long time.

The *Cormorant* was well supplied; fresh fruit and bread would last several days, eggs a few days longer and then he would supplement canned foods, hard biscuits and cereals with fresh fish, he hoped. The wind vane had worked well during trials and was like having another crewmember that never slept. He had a sextant, compass, charts and a fascinating atlas that showed the ocean bottom. Departure had been delayed as he waited for a stable mid-Atlantic high. He planned to follow the Great Circle Route to Newfoundland to take advantage of favourable currents south of Greenland and in the Labrador Sea.

The first week was idyllic; the wind vane steered, the breeze was fair and the tiny trailing impellor of the Walker Log recorded an average of 92 miles a day. Wilhelm could only sleep an hour or two at a time and a mild fatigue began. In the lonely watches the mists of depression and guilt that had plagued his past swirled about. He had avoided bringing alcohol, another enemy over the years. Manic depression, alcoholism and amnesia, the Doctor had written.

On the ninth day the atlas showed that he was suspended in waters that were two and one half miles deep, approaching the foothills of the Mid Atlantic Ridge, which rose ten thousand feet from the deepest plain. He imagined that tiny cable, stretching across submerged mountains, canyons and plains all the way from Valencia to a tiny Outport in Newfoundland. What arrogance indeed!

The next day a huge fish splashed astern, swallowed his impellor and snapped the Walker Log line. The barometer was dropping and he prepared for weather. By 2 a.m., the wind was force eight. He spent the night on the wheel as the quartering seas were too much for the wind vane. All in all, *Cormorant* seemed to like his adjustments and the boisterous assault on his senses improved his mood. The blow was short lived and was replaced by a light north-westerly and clear weather.

Awakening from a nap at 2.45 p.m. on the thirteenth day at sea he studied his chart and realized, with a sudden discomfort in his gut, that his position, 56 degrees N, and 23 degrees S, was close, very close, to where U694 had sunk the passenger ship Sirius on Nov.3, 1941. He recalled that late afternoon 40 years ago as if it were yesterday, no amnesia there. He was the torpedo officer. They had come upon the Sirius by pure chance and were lying in her path. He remembered the order to fire, the long wait, and then the low rumbling sound like distant thunder that was drowned out by the cheering crew. He had several press clippings; 326 people were lost including 32 English children being evacuated to Canada. He looked at the gray seas and shivered with anguish. Miles below, on the side of a volcanic mountain or in the mud of a valley floor were the bones of 326 innocents. They had cheered and were given medals! Could there be a more awful crime, a greater obscenity? To rupture the hull of a ship which was home and hope for hundreds of human beings and send them in terror to a slow, merciless death in dark frigid waters. How could other human beings, who loved and dreamed, commit and celebrate such an act? He had long thought and read and written on the dark psychology of man. Wilhelm leaned forward with his arms on the coach roof and wept.

For the next few days *Cormorant* sailed on, she was captain and the wind vane was crew. Wilhelm roused himself occasionally to adjust the vane but otherwise succumbed to sleep deprivation, malnourishment and the ravages of depression. *Cormorant* sailed on 200 miles north of the Flemish Cap, an outrider of the Grand Banks of Newfoundland. The days were gray and cold.

One morning, fumbling for consciousness, he became aware of a strange light; golden cones were coming horizontally through the starboard portholes and shining on the opposite bulkheads; the cabin was diffused with brightness. *Cormorant* was quiet, but he heard soft sounds like breaking waves. Alarmed, he stumbled up the companionway steps. There, 100 yards to the northeast, was a huge iceberg, with seas washing white on a green base. A lens-like sheet of ice on the berg's flank was reflecting a cone of light from the morning sun directly on *Cormorant*. The boat's shadow was lying to the south. The beauty of the scene charmed him. He felt enthralled; a tide moved in his consciousness. He watched the changing light as he sailed out of danger, then for the first time in weeks, he had an urge for music and turned on his record player and listened to *Tannhauser*.

The humpback was following a capelin school through seas now changing from dawn gray to the bluish tones of sunrise. His sonar followed the capelin mass as it dived deeper now, thousands of lives rolling in a capelin cloud, numbers and togetherness reducing the chance of individual predation. Yesterday the great whale had cruised bays and coves, but overnight had moved some twenty miles offshore. Straight ahead was the sluicing hull of a sailboat.

Wilhelm saw the whale on the splendid canvas of sea and sky. He watched the graceful power as the mammal rolled through a breaking wave and thrust its great tail skyward before sinking into the depths just a few yards back in the boat's wake.

Wilhelm was gaunt, with a ragged gray beard now showing only traces of red. Only shards of depression remained. A pattern had developed during the past 22 days at sea. What a strange blend was solo sailing! All that he was and could be was here in this small space. His tiny turf must be defended against the nonchalant power of the sea: vigilance; constant attention to gear and rigging; preparation of food; conservation of energy; the battle against cold and damp; always assessing the mood of opposing seas and sky; plotting direction, speed and position.

He inspected the steering wind vane while eating a pickled egg, marvelling at the ingenuity of the device that kept his little ship sailing at a set angle to the wind. Fixes on the chart marched westward from Valencia in Ireland indicating he was about 22 miles off the south coast of Newfoundland. A quiet euphoria feuded with fatigue. His ego received sustenance from having so far survived the implacable North Atlantic.

During the morning, he gazed westward through eyes opaque with age. It was 13:00 hours and the great island was only 12 nautical miles away when he first saw blue coastal hills. Petrels skimmed the waves and shearwaters disappeared into troughs. His chart showed deep water close inshore. He hove to, brewed coffee and washed in warm water. He stowed gear and prepared mooring lines and fenders.

By 1500 hours, the cutter *Cormorant* lay becalmed off Fortune Harbour. With batteries dead and exhausted from spinning the flywheel of the reluctant 10 hp diesel, Wilhelm Prostner sat and looked at the square, multi-coloured houses and listened to the distant sounds of children and dogs. He was hailed by a passing fisherman and soon was being towed up the harbour and secured alongside in a bustle of helping hands and gathering villagers.

"My son, where ar' ya from? Oh Ir'land, is it! Good for you! What's your name? Donald Cadger you say? No one be da name of Badger 'round 'ere … oh sorry! Cadger you say. Well you're a bit t'in, I'd say a double-barrelled twelve-gauge shotgun would make you a good pair o' pants; just fit it would. Well c'mon b'y. Da women will fatten you up I allows."

Now he is secure. An outport woman brings him pea soup. He surrenders to exhaustion and falls into his bunk. The boat's conversation at sea, the creak and wind song of shrouds, the cadence of bow waves, the rudder sluice; all have been replaced by the occasional creaking of mooring lines. He remembers the exuberance of starry skies and moonlight, the malevolent foreboding of black nights. His brain, screaming for repair, repulses incoming sensation and falls into the realm of sleep. Now, lacking the control of consciousness, images are retrieved randomly from memory and grow, with association, into dreams … The Kapitan, seemingly suspended in his black uniform, holds the periscope handles with both hands.

"Speed 15 knots. Distance 1800 metres. Prepare No. 2 tube."

"Slight left rudder."

"Fire!"

There is a rumbling recoil, then silence. Waiting—then, a distant explosion. Wilhelm is suddenly with women and children in watery chaos. The triumphant shouts of the U boat crew mingle with the screams of terror and pain from mothers and children. Violent water. Debris of steel and wood. Bodies float by. The lovely face of a child swims towards him, fixes him with a look of ultimate betrayal, then the face contorts to twisted flesh and blood. He awakens with a shout, and lies in the dark, his heart pounding. How can this be? How can this happen? What madness rules? How can one species inflict such terror upon innocents of its own kind? Is it because the misery we create—the pain, suffering, humiliation, indignity does not accumulate, but seems to disappear with each individual into the sea, or ground, or gas chamber? How can we be so easily led to develop ferocious hatred for our own, to applaud the infliction of heinous wounds and death? He was part of this!

He was born in Scotland, and remembers misty seacoasts and dark hills. He loved and drew strength from his childhood. He was guiltless then and the future lay pristine and promising before him. Then his Father, Herman Prostner, who was with a German firm in Edinburgh, moved back to Berlin in 1930. Wilhelm was 16 years old. He was sent to a State school and came to consider himself a German. He was caught in the geyser of political madness that would strangle the struggling themes of European democracy.

He read *Mein Kampf* and joined the Nazi youth. He was also caught in the silken web of German music, an acoustic renaissance that culminated in the nationalist sagas of Wagner and the beckoning philosophy of Nietzsche.

The German Secret Service sent him to Oxford in 1938 as a student spy, named Donald Cadger, after his Mother's maiden name. He joined the Navy, volunteered for the submarine service and was posted to U694 under Capitan Helmut Schultz. U694 was given the special mission of interrupting the flow of information between Britain and North America via the transatlantic cable. This cable connected Valencia in Ireland to Heart's Content in Newfoundland. Wilhelm was sent to the German Embassy in Dublin, where he could move about freely. He studied the cable station at Valencia, memorizing its design and technology, which was apparently similar to the one in Heart's Content.

Ten days out of Ireland the black dreams had begun, and the fearful remembrance of what he had witnessed and aided, had awakened the bear of depression. It crept over him like twilight. Some part of his brain supplied quantum energy that altered the neurotransmitters. He could feel the blinds being drawn. He considered the desolation of humanity. Insanity seemed to prevail in individuals, provinces, nations, and the planet. Vast expanses of the exquisite human brain were captive of cults, isms and religions that led it into behaviours devoid of mercy, capable of inflicting the most vicious injury on one and all.

So he plumbed the depths of despair while the ocean looked on, changing from the luminosity of day to the fluorescence of night. It was light and Wagner's music that began to lift his brain's chemical veil. By the time he was towed into harbour, the memory of what had happened on these rugged coasts filled him with grief, but not depression.

The next morning, a foggy sun found the *Cormorant's* portholes. She was moored to the side of a fish flake in the center of outport activity. Fishermen cleaned cod in a flux of gulls. Children gathered to gaze and giggle. Seal carcasses lay on the harbour bottom. A summer breeze wafted the perfume of clover. The gas station-grocery store-restaurant was just 100 yards away.

CHAPTER 34

▼

Five years had passed since the *Cormorant* tied up in Fortune. Newfoundland, guarding the eastern approaches to North America, lay in peace, a land rich in forests and rivers, with treasures of oil and minerals. Set in a living sea, it was intimate with its people in a mutual love affair.

To return to these rugged coasts had become an obsession with Wilhelm, an obsession that had survived alcoholism, amnesia and depression, a psychic hope that to revisit would heal. But he must be true to himself and here he was still using Douglas Cadger as an alias; the demon lived on!

Wilhelm was now embedded in the life of the village. He still lived on *Cormorant* but had bought a cabin on a nearby river where he lived for several months each year. He fished salmon, joined the Wildflower Association and often walked the magnificent coastal trails. He became friends with several families, especially with the children. He had given a scholarship to the local school and had bought a sailing dingy on which he gave lessons. Wilhelm was considered an exotic character and a favourite in the outport.

Mostly, however, he read, wrote and thought. He was intrigued by the rise of Fascism in Germany. By what strange process could democratic Germany become mesmerized by an inhuman racist dictator? What were the seeds? Was it the nationalism of Bismarck, Darwinian concepts, Nietschean philosophy, and Wagnerian music? Durant had written: *'Out of the Dionysian root of the German spirit a power had arisen, namely German music, in its vast solar orbit from Bach to Beethoven to Wagner. Wagner fused all this into aesthetic synthesis.'* Music, surely, must be a minor piece in this great puzzle, the enigma of man's inhumanity to man.

Sometimes he felt like he was reliving the pleasure and innocence of childhood, but he knew that to complete his journey, to dampen the searing flame of guilt, he had to visit one place. He had not yet found the courage, even though he had met a woman from Heart's Content and they had become good friends. The meeting was not really by accident. He had attended a psychology lecture at the university in St. John's and afterwards a woman had asked a question, identifying herself as being from Heart's Content. He had gone over and introduced himself as Donald Cadger. She was a mature psychology student, a feminist and hungrily interested in education. They corresponded and occasionally met at the University.

CHAPTER 35

▼

Their wedding anniversary was in two days. Matt and Vanessa sat in the living room of their new house and reminisced.

"Where did the four years go?" asked Vanessa, "and sure it has been two years since you resigned from the Biotech Company and set up your own practice."

"I haven't regretted the decision for a minute. My practice is so much more interesting and the 45-minute drive to the medical school is no problem; it gives me time to relax and think."

"So much has happened in those four years: Nigel completing his PhD in physics at Cambridge; Jonathan graduating and getting a job with the National Research Council in Ottawa. I sure hope he gets that position he has applied for with Newfoundland Hydro."

"And Nigel—what a bright fellow! He's between both sailboats and girlfriends at the moment; must have time on his hands!"

"And all the gang is well."

"Especially Rachel. Isn't she a wonder? Sam's death, then the pituitary tumour, and then she went back to school to get her grade eleven. Now she's got the wind in her tail and who knows where she will end up!"

"Now you won't believe what Sarah told me about Rachel," said Vanessa.

"Oh?"

"She said Rachel has a man friend whom she met at the University. Said he was old enough to be her father."

"Really!"

"Sarah said Tom hadn't said much about it, which was strange, until one day he looked up and said 'Mom was like a bird in a cage; she didn't know what her feathers were for; then she got out b'y and started flappin' 'er wings. Now she's flyin' 'round like a storm petrel!'"

"Tom says he's 'all crippled up wonderful wit d'art'ritis,' but he still manages to pursue a love/hunt relationship with just about every creature on land and sea."

"It is disappointing that there has been nothing further on the Heart's Content mystery, nothing on W.P. since his cousin told us he had left for Ireland," said Vanessa.

"The police say more secret German war documents will be released next year. Maybe we should go to Greece and track down the cousin. That seems to be the only lead."

"How are the plans coming for next year's get together?"

"Well, as you know, Jonathan has been appointed a committee of one. I was talking to him Tuesday and he said all the usual suspects are coming plus some of their friends. He's planning on a week late in the lobster season. First, we will hike in the Anguille Mountains, spend a day or two at Gros Morne, and then convene at some local resort. Man! So much is happening in so many scientific fields. And the social chaos is mind-boggling. Just heard that there has been another religious massacre in India, and there are at least seven wars in Africa, even in areas of famine."

"Oh the poor Planet. Like the fellar said, "Da ass is out of 'er b'y!""

"Let's have a drink!"

CHAPTER 36

▼

The following summer, Matt arranged to exchange practices with a G.P. from Fortune, as he wanted to explore the Burin peninsula and do some salmon fishing in the Conne River that flowed into Bay D'Espoir. He also wanted to get the reaction of the locals to the finding of the wreck of the *Blackduck* near Heart's Content, which had intensified rather than solved the mystery.

Matt's first call took him to a yellow house with a picket fence in need of whitewashing. He followed Elizabeth Bryant upstairs, where her sister Amy lay near a window that overlooked the harbour. A vase of dandelion flowers smiled from a bedside table.

"Ailin' she's been all winter and not a scrap of appetite."

Amy was apologetic about bothering the doctor. They chatted for a minute about the weather and the late blooming of the lilacs. Examination revealed a hard, fixed nodule in the left breast, an enlarged irregular liver and evidence of marked weight loss.

Matt followed Elizabeth down the stairs. She was robust and rounded, but still resembled her sister who lay emaciated in the room above. She stopped by the piano that was their sole source of income and managed a brave voice.

"It's bad, isn't it, Doctor?"

"I'm afraid so," he answered in a voice an octave too low. "Most likely a breast tumour that has spread to the liver. In that case, not much we can do. But let's see what the tests show."

He sat at the kitchen table, which was covered with oilcloth depicting images of tall ships, and wrote instructions while Elizabeth trembled inside. "Will you 'ave a cup a tea Doctor?"

"Not now thanks, but I'll come by after the investigation and then we will chat and have tea." He walked toward the car, considering with chagrin the number of diseases still defying scientific medicine.

A young boy thumped up in rubber boots.

"Ar' you the Doctor, sir?"

"Hello, yes."

"Der's a sick old feller down on his boat me dad wants you to see."

Matt had noted with interest the mast behind the fish flake. Now he stood beside a cutter that showed the effects of climate and time but looked snugly secure in her berth.

"Been 'ere since several summers," said the boy's father. "Sailed 'ere all the way from Ireland 'e did. All by 'is self. Interesting old guy, got to be good friends wit many people around 'ere. 'E was always 'ale and 'arty but 'as been failin' for weeks and can barely crawl over the rail now. Glad you're 'ere Doc."

"Permission to come aboard?"

"Granted," a weak voice from below decks replied.

Matt climbed over the safety lines and down the companionway. Bacon and eggs lay old and cold on the gas stove. Gear was strewn about. A bearded man lay in the starboard berth, his face pale in the dim light. The air was stale.

"I'm Dr. Penwell."

"Donald Cadger." A low voice and a trembling handshake.

"So you sailed her across alone? Congrats. That makes you special."

"Special, indeed," he said with a wry smile.

"Tell me about yourself."

"Thought I had the flu but I can't shake it, it's shaking me."

Matt examined the man and reviewed the history. Examination revealed a blowing grade III mitral valve murmur, a slightly enlarged liver and a fever of 38.5°C. A small linear haemorrhage was present under a fingernail.

"I've lost a lot of weight and have no appetite."

Matt thought he detected a slight European accent.

"Well, there are several possibilities. Most likely, you have an infection. I'll admit you to the hospital for studies."

"Interesting craft," said Matt, looking around. He noted the book-case: *The Search for Schrödinger's Cat*, A biography of Wagner. He picked up, *River out of Eden*, which was covered with mildew. "Oh, sorry," he said, "I'm being forward, but I like your library."

The old man smiled.

The fisherman was waiting when Matt climbed over the *Cormorant*'s safety lines.

"'Ow 'is 'e, doc?"

"Quite ill, I suspect. I'll be admitting him to hospital."

"'E's been real friends with the Blaine family over in the cove. They'll keep an eye on the craft. Use our phone if you like, we're just down th' road 'ere."

Matt phoned and had the ambulance dispatched to take the old sailor to hospital.

Hours later, Matt sat sipping a scotch and sifting the ashes of the day. In the western sky the sun had found a break in a tumble of low cloud and was sending a tepee of light down to the shining sea.

That old Captain is interesting medically, he mused, and he obviously has a story to tell. How about his library? I look forward to knowing him better. He was just turning on a Beatles record when the phone rang.

"Dr. Penwell. Mr. Cadger has taken a turn. His speech is difficult and he says he can't see. His temperature is 102."

"Thanks. Be right over."

"His speech is better," the nurse greeted when he arrived. "He's been quite delirious and rambling on about submarines and secret codes."

The examination was unchanged.

"Probably had a T.I.A. or a small embolus," thought Matt.

"Let's do another blood culture and put him on an antiplatelet medicine. Anything from bacteriology?'

"No, we should have it in the morning."

Next morning Cadger remained febrile and weak but speech and vision had returned.

"Were you a submariner?"

Cadger moved a hand quickly.

"Yes, I was in the Navy, both on the surface and below."

"That's interesting. One doesn't hear much about the British submarine service. The Germans stole that show, I guess."

"You could say that," Cadger murmured, closed his eyes and laid his head back on the pillow.

"Oh, here are the lab reports," said the nurse.

"Anemia. Leukocytosis. Hey, a positive blood culture. Look at this. Streptococcus Bovis. That's a rare one! Good news, it's sensitive to penicillin. The diagnosis is bacterial endocarditis. What a great case! Where did he get that bug?"

Matt called a colleague at the medical school in St. John's. Dr. Young sounded enthused.

"Most unusual. Strep Bovis is quite a new pathogen. Just heard about it at a conference a few months ago. One can catch it from unpasteurized cheese or milk. The bug gets into the blood stream through a tumour in the bowel and then sets up shop on the heart valves. Good for you. Hey, you've made my day. He'll be a celebrity here at Health Sciences. I'll arrange a bed."

CHAPTER 37

▼

Matt paused a moment before knocking on the door of the red ochre house. He glanced down the steep back garden, with its small lilacs and gooseberries, to a rocky path leading to the weathered wharf. A white rowboat of perfect contour reflected in the dark water.

"Yes, sir."

"Good morning. I'm Dr. Penwell. I've come to see you, not about medicine, but about the mystery of the *Blackduck*."

"Sure, come on in. I knows you. You found the arm in Trinity Bay. Isaac," she called. "It's the Doctor to see us about Jed."

They sat at the kitchen table.

"He was a fine lad," said Isaac, "if we just knew what happened, it would make it easier for us all. We also lost a nephew, Adam Cotter, who was studying to be an engineer."

Sadie put the kettle on and returned with a large album.

"Jed's sister kept a scrap book of all the goin's on, pictures and police reports and so on."

"What do you know for sure?" asked Matt.

"Well b'y. Dey left Fortune at 7:00 a.m., a fine healthy bunch. Put into St. Pierre. Apparently there were some ructions d'ere dat night, over girls, whatever. Dey left St. Pierre 6:00 a.m. next day for the Banks. Never seen hide nor hair again. Nuttin' at all. First we were sure it was the Frenchies. Sure, den dey found 'er near Heart's Content, and a man's arm that belonged to a Nazi submariner, but the man whose initials were on dat arm turned out to be alive somewhere. Nobody can find him. It's a great mystery for sure. None of de boy's bodies were ever found. D'er were seven families bereaved and we're still sufferin' a generation later. Sure, I'm an old man and I still can't put it out of my mind."

Matt studied the scrapbook and a picture of the *Blackduck*.

"This man looks familiar," said Matt, looking at a black and white snapshot of an old man holding a blond child's hand.

"Dat's old Captain Cadger who lives on the *Cormorant* down in the harbour. Been there for years. He's a good friend and takes a great interest in Jed's sons."

"Oh, right. I'm just looking after him now."

"Yeah, he looked sick lately. Hope he's ok."

"Being treated," said Matt. "Have the Mounties been here? Is the case still alive?"

"Yes, b'y. Not 'tree weeks ago, Sadie was talkin' to a Mountie and 'e told about de new documents comin' out in Berlin and dey are still lookin'."

Matt finished his tea, borrowed a photo of the *Blackduck* and said his farewells.

"Nice to meet you Doc. Drop in anytime you're hereabouts. Yes, b'y."

Matt made rounds. He felt an unusual rapport with old Cadger. Here was obviously an interesting character with many stories. Listening to the heart, he heard the four muscular cylinders rushing blood through the open valves, which then stopped the blood from returning by closing when the chambers relaxed. Over the mitral valve, however, was a returning blood rush, a murmur, indicating a damaged valve.

He explained the rare diagnosis to the Captain saying that he had a bacterial heart valve infection with valve damage: the probable presence of a bowel tumour and the necessity of prolonged intravenous antibiotic treatment.

"Have you eaten any unpasteurized cheese?"

"That's a funny question. Actually, I'm a fan of cheese and you can get great cheese here, would you believe? Imported from St. Pierre just a few miles away."

"Any aboard the *Cormorant* now?"

"Probably."

"Permission to look aboard her?"

"Yes," and a hesitant, "of course. Will I make it Doctor?"

"You have a serious illness. We need more studies to hone the prognosis. However, we have the means to eradicate the infection and the tumour, so your chances of survival are reasonable."

"Doctor, I have no one. I have written a letter. It's on *Cormorant*, hidden in a book—*The Origin of Species*. Please take it. Not to be opened until my death."

They shook hands.

This time the *Cormorant* looked forlorn and neglected in the drizzling rain. Seagulls had decorated her foredeck. Matt slid back the companionway hatch and went below. It was dampish and smelled of mildew. He stood for a moment feeling reverence for the little ship, the clinging silence broken only by wavelets slapping the hull. He looked at the bookcase: '*English Romantic Poets*', '*Old Man and the Sea*', John Ruskin's, '*King of the Golden River*'. He picked out '*The Origin of Species*'. A newspaper clipping fell out. It was in German, dated Berlin, and seemed to be reporting the death of a German submarine commander. A stained letter was taped inside the back cover. He put the book back. Inside the musty icebox was a half consumed package of Touree de l'Aubier! "Eureka!" he thought. He read the fine print—indeed it was unpasteurized—imported from France via the Island of St. Pierre. "Ah the French," he thought, "they produce a Pasteur and then ignore his advice." He put a sample of the cheese in a glass tube for bacteriology.

The v-berth was a mess. Matt poked about and was about to leave when he noticed something under the chart table. "Ah, his sextant," he thought. He opened the dusty mahogany case and gently removed the instrument. It was an expensive German Zeiss. It seemed familiar for some reason. In the bottom of the case was a crumpled piece of paper. He picked it out and saw stained handwriting. He walked over to the porthole light and adjusted his glasses. "Looks like Spanish," he thought. The first word was Wilhelm, and then farther along he saw the word 'sextant' followed by an eight-digit number. It was signed Maria. What? Matt gasped with a wild surmise! He sat down on the companionway steps. It is—it has to be the sextant I saw in Vall-demossa.

C H A P T E R   38

▼

Jonathan and Betty sat having a cocktail in their living room. They
had been married almost three years. Betty worked at a small tech
company in St. John's. They had just returned from hiking on the
East Coast Trail near Flatrock. The window looked out on grassland,
which was dotted with crouching tuckamores and sloped to the cliff's
edge some 200 feet above the sea. A portion of pebble beach could be
seen edging cliffs rising steeply to form the northern boundary of the
cove.

"I have a meeting on Tuesday with the natural resources minister
on the Churchill Falls project. They are planning to challenge the
upper Churchill Agreement in the Supreme Court. I like to concen-
trate on engineering and avoid politics, but this agreement is so
bizarre. It, in effect, makes us energy slaves to Quebec for 70 years.
We get about three percent of the profits out of which we have to
maintain the plant and deliver the power to the Quebec border."

"Bizarre," said Betty, who had Nova Scotian roots, "I'm reading
Joey Smallwood's Memoirs—as you requested sir!" she saluted. "A
truly amazing character—a loquacious dynamo who certainly sought
out the rich and famous. He also had a malady that I've run into a few
times in this Province—a bad case of 'touch your hat' anglophilia.
Maybe that had something to do with the Churchill Falls negotiations."

"Hey great! I'm most interested in your opinions. The sequence of negotiations is confusing as I remember. I'm sure he left a lot out of the memoir."

"Well," Betty replied, "he certainly was aware of what he was up against with Quebec. Listen to this quote from page 460—'I was convinced that Quebec would show neither scruple or conscience in its treatment of Newfoundland—that we would be victimized at every turn.'"

"Prophetic indeed," Jonathan said. "So because Quebec would not allow transmission of Labrador power across its territory to the U.S. the idea of an all Anglo Saxon route was raised—Labrador-Newfoundland-Nova Scotia-U.S.—and this was deemed feasible, but only if Newfoundland would nationalize Churchill Falls as Quebec had done earlier with its hydro industry."

"Right," Betty said, "but Joey would not nationalize because that would have damaged the English interests that had done so much of the original work. See, his anglophilia intervened."

"And his sense of fair play and propriety, you might add. The Federal Government had the legal power to force Quebec to allow transmission lines to cross to the U.S., but they lacked the courage. It's said that Joey went secretly to Ottawa to request this of Prime Minister Pearson, but Pearson asked Joey not to make a formal request because Canada could not protect the power lines. That's where Joey goofed—let us down—he should have insisted!"

"Hey, if you could find documentation of that you should have a case for the courts indeed."

"Then Joey seemed to suddenly submit and seem delighted with a disastrous deal—a forty year agreement with no provision for escalating costs and profits! And then, at the last moment Quebec demanded and got a further 25-year extension with Newfoundland's share actually reduced, if you can believe that. It seems hard to get info on the details of that insane extension. Actually several of the Newfoundland negotiators were killed in a plane crash a few weeks after the agreement was signed."

"Bizarre," said Betty, "bizarre again! Didn't you have any lawyers? Were they all on pot? That deal meant the difference between prosperity and humiliating subservience for Newfoundland. So what's to be done—is there an option left?"

"They are taking the case to the Supreme Court. If that fails, as I think it will, I'd take it to the United Nations and if that fails I'll tell you what I would do, I'd ..." The telephone interrupted their conversation.

"Hey Jonathan, it's Matt."

"Yes, b'y."

"Some interesting happenings down here on the Burin peninsula. I'm coming to St. John's on Wednesday. May we have lunch?"

"No problem. We have some catching up to do, hey, you sound excited, what's up?"

"Tell you Wednesday—you'll be so taken you'll probably want to pay the tab."

"See you at lunch."

On Wednesday, Matt and Jonathan were escorted to a table overlooking the old city of St. John's. The port was in sunlight but fog paws poked in through the narrows and a foghorn moaned from Fort Townsend. A black and white pilot boat directed ships like a border collie, herding sheep.

Matt could barely contain himself while they both ordered pan-fried cod.

"Wow! Something remarkable is unfolding."

"What's happening?" asked Jonathan, surprised by the excitement in Matt's voice.

"First of all, I have a rare medical diagnosis, most likely the first case ever diagnosed on the Rock. Secondly, I may have found the central figure in the mystery of the bones we found off Heart's Content, and all in the person of one Captain Cadger of the good ship *Cormorant*." Matt proceeded to tell the story of the last few days in Fortune.

Jonathan, eyebrows raised, sampled his scrunchins.

"So, let's see. We have an old sailor who made it to Fortune from the cable port, Valencia, in Ireland. He is interested in the survivors of the dead fishermen, and there is evidence he was connected to the Nazi sub service."

"Oh yes. He admits that."

"And you think the sextant on the *Cormorant* is the one you saw in Valldemossa? C'mon Matt, that was years ago."

"Well I can't prove it, but I'm quite sure it is. And there was the note signed Maria."

"That's right, and remember the man we phoned in Navpaktos said his brother had gone to Ireland and was talking about some frozen place in the northern seas?"

"Hey, this is too much, but it does seem to add up. Will he survive your fancy disease?"

"Ah. We have to battle the bugs, catch the cancer and then mend the mitral. A 50% chance, I would say. The echocardiogram showed a large thrombus streaming back and forth in the mitral flow. It could break off any minute and stroke him, but we are trying to prevent that."

"What do we do now?"

"That's a dilemma. As his doctor, there's the confidentiality thing, and I quite like the old guy. But the answer to the mystery of the bones and the *Blackduck* is likely at our fingertips."

They sat silently for a few minutes, sipping coffee and watching passengers disembark from a cruise ship docked on Harbour Drive.

"Let's see. We could search the yacht for more clues."

"And you could question him further, perhaps confront him with your suspicions."

"I wouldn't want to upset him at this stage of the disease."

"Sooner or later, we will have to call the Royal Newfoundland Constabulary."

"Well by the Lord dyin' sufferin' b'y, we've got a big one hooked for sure."

"What's with you?"

"Same old," said Jonathan, "except, some people are wondering how Newfoundland was short circuited so that we get nothing from Churchill Falls and I'm involved in that."

"Hey, there's a cause celeb! Go for it! Our annual trek-chat fest is in Gros Morne in September. Nigel's coming. Right now, he's negotiating to buy a 40' Rival Bowman. He plans to sail across for the big meeting at Heart's Content in two years time. Everybody seems keen and preparing."

"Yes, b'y," Jonathan smiled wryly. "The soiree at Heart's Content is when you and I publish a book that will explain everything in layman's English. At least we'll have Tom there to leaven the loaf of knowledge."

"Is there a place in hell reserved for hubristic Newfoundlanders?" smiled Matt, as they parted.

CHAPTER 39

▼

"Dr. Mallam has found a tumour in the sigmoid colon," said the nurse. "He wants to talk to cardiology."

Captain Cadger lay pale and gaunt, tube tied to a small white island surrounded by machines that blinked red and green eyes. Matt explained the colon cancer and the need for surgery.

"Just a few more tests, old-timer," He said. "You should be ready for surgery in a few days. Do you have any relatives?"

"None."

"Nurse said you talked about a brother."

Cadger looked startled. "Well, there was a brother in Greece—much older—certainly long dead now."

Matthew stifled an in-breath. "There it was! Surely the answers to the mystery lay in that septic old body before him. I need to think," thought Matthew. "I'll go for a walk."

The trail led below the cliff at Fort Waldegrave and on through the old fishing village of the Outer Battery. On his left, in varying poses, houses nestled into the cliff face, while to his right skeletons of old fishing flakes stood greyly defiant, with feet in the sea. Matt walked past shore batteries built to defy U-boats and sea raiders of World War II. He left the main trail and climbed down near the sea. He sat down in a soft micro valley of mosses and blackberries. Each gaze was rewarded with most magnificent coastal scenery, including Cape

Spear to the southeast and the eternal mystery of a sea horizon. Just below him, the waves surged blue, then green, to foaming white in a Brahamian cadence.

His mind was restless, like the sea. He recalled the O.R. scene with the team operating on old Cadger. There had been anxious moments during induction of anaesthesia, but soon the heart-lung machine was pumping and a scalpel cut through the fibrillating left auricular wall of the crimson heart, exposing the bileaflet mitral valve which sat like a bishop's mitre, normally controlling flow between the low pressure left auricle and the high pressure left ventricle. They looked with great interest at the polypoid mass that protruded like black current jelly from the anterior leaflet. This was carefully removed, revealing a 1-cm. hole in the leaflet where Strep Bovis had fed. A patch was cut from that silken gown, the pericardium, which ensheathes the heart, and the hole repaired.

Cadger had recovered well and was now ready to be discharged from intensive care.

"So what do I do now?" thought Matt. "He's my friend and patient and he's almost certainly a German submariner who may know something about the wreck of the *Blackduck*. It just has to be! Should he call the R.N.C.?"

Matt had revisited Burin and found an old man in a red shed filled with trophies of the sea who was the brother of the mate of the ill-fated schooner. He told of the struggle to raise four children who became orphans when the mother died just two years after the Schooner's disappearance. He also told of becoming friends with Cadger who had shown great interest in the children and had helped them in many ways.

Matt rolled over on his back, looked up into the blue universe and listened to the sounds of this coastal Eden. "Right." he thought, "sort this out now. The mystery must be solved and justice done. I'll face him with it."

He entered the hospital, his senses on high alert. He noted taupe walls with flowered paper strips at eye level attempting cheerfulness.

Beige curtains with vertical ripples of varying wavelengths fostering privacy; monitors with the secret electrical life of the heart trudging from left to right; bags of liquid, like huge teardrops, hanging from poles and emitting plastic tentacles which disappeared into rumpled bodies. Linear lights cast a cadaveric glow over all. Through a window, he glimpsed fog pushing its grey menace through the narrows. His mood was now dark, alert.

Captain Cadger was asleep. His thin body seemed painted in recline. His carotid arteries pulsed regularly. A bony left arm, showing bruises in varying stages of absorption, welcomed the I.V.

"Ah, the good doctor," said Cadger, after a slight shove on the bed had awakened cloudy blue eyes.

Matt smiled and busied himself for a moment with the bedside chart. "Vitals are good. How are you feeling?"

"Stronger. I walked. Craving some food. I ate better crossing the Atlantic. I guess it is all the good stuff is in that white drink they keep bringing."

Matt sighed, dismissed the nurse and sat down.

"Listen old timer," he intoned. "I have a story I must tell you because I think you may have been one of the actors in it."

He told of finding the arm on the beach, of the bracelet with the initials, W.P., the number 694 and the crooked cross. He recounted the mystery of the disappearance of the *Blackduck* and of Tom's finding the wreck nearby. He told how release of German documents had revealed that U694 had been in these waters, of his telephone call to Navpaktos, and of his suspicions upon meeting Cadger and searching the *Cormorant* in Burin.

At first, Cadger's face became fixed and impassive. His body seemed even smaller on the sheets. Matt noted the carotid pulse was faster. When Matt finished there was silence. Cadger looked out at the now foggy early twilight. Then he turned to Matt and a smile spread slowly over his countenance, while liquid sparkled on closed lids.

Matt rose and put a hand on his shoulder. "I'm still your friend and your doctor."

"I'm overwhelmed. I've been living with this for a lifetime. It's twisted me in so many ways … I had a long period when alcohol was my friend and sometimes black depression. It's true, what you imply … but it's not true. What a relief, you've figured it out. Why did I conceal it all these years? I feel happy, euphoric, now it will all come out. Am I guilty or not? I have tried to understand, have consulted the world's leading minds in books. Why is man so incorrigible? You must do what you must do. Thank you my friend. Please call the authorities."

CHAPTER 40

▼

The lobster season was open. Pack ice and icebergs from the glaciers of Greenland floated south on the plankton-rich Arctic current. Life stirred—great flocks of seabirds, puffins, murrs, and gannets returning to coastal islands for food and nesting. Matt and Jonathan were spending a weekend with Tom to help with the lobsters and do some speckled trout fishing. Tom's sons had 80 pots set in the bay and today's catch totalled 56 lobsters, three of which now lay steaming red in a pot by the fire.

"Now b'y," said Tom "Isn't this some goin' on about this fellar Cadger. I'm sure I'm goin' to get the details right now from you two. I've a clipping 'ere from the Telegram ... you read it Jonathan."

Jonathan read, '*Today in this city by the springtime sea, embers of the great conflagration of WWII were rekindled. The dramatic trial of Wilhelm Prostner, alias Captain Cadger, has thrown a revealing light, not only on the wartime exploits of German submarines, but also on one of the most baffling sea mysteries that has been part of our storied culture for half a century*'.

"We know most of the details of his background, no doubt, from the news stories," said Matt, "but I have a tape you'll find riveting for sure. To review briefly, he was born in Scotland of German parents. His father worked for Siemens Corp. The family moved back to Berlin in 1930 when he was 16. He was caught up in the fervour of the

Nazi Youth movement. When his parents objected, he ran away from home and joined the Hitler Youth. He joined the German navy in 1938 and the submarine service in 1939. He said that two kills in the North Atlantic appalled him at the loss of innocent life. He was landed from a sub at Dublin Ireland in 1940 to get data on the Anglo American Cable station at Valencia. There, he says, he contacted MI-5 and became a double agent with the code name, Tristan. The German plan was to destroy the cables and cable station at Heart's Content, Newfoundland and so interrupt the main communications between Brita in and North America. Can you believe it? We were the targets! How unaware we were."

"Well b'y, they did have a blackout in effect, I remember."

"Anyway," said Matt, "Here's Cadger's story, on tape."

We ran on the surface all night, charging our batteries. At dawn on June 14th, 1941, Lieutenant-Commander Karl Prien took U694 down to periscope level. Our position was 22 miles S.S.E. off Cape Race, Newfoundland. At 9:20 p.m., the mist cleared and revealed a schooner under full sail about five miles away.

Prepare to surface and ready assault craft, ordered the Captain.

We came alongside. The fishermen's faces showed fear and amazement except for one young giant who seemed unfazed. The boarding party rushed below but there was no wireless. The crew was rounded up on the quarterdeck. A search for weapons found several 12 gauge shotguns and 22 calibre rifles used to hunt birds and seals.

"Obey all orders or you will be shot immediately," the crew were told.

Diving equipment and other supplies were being transferred to the schooner when a plane's engines were heard and the U-boat quickly submerged.

Lt. Schultz was in command. The boarding party was ordered to get the Blackduck underway. We sailed all day.

By nightfall, we were off Baccalieu Island at the entrance to Trinity Bay. During the night, under diesel, we followed the lights of outports along the shore and by dawn, June 15th, we were anchored near an inlet called Seal Cove, just W.S.W. of the harbour of Heart's Content.

The crew seemed docile but sullen, except for this youth of about 19 years who was huge, handsome and radiated energy and fearlessness. He was irrepressible, it seemed. He appeared wearing a shirt made of a Union Jack. He offered me his watch for my U694 bracelet identification and proudly wore the souvenir. I kept looking at his vigorous and graceful movements. Lt. Schultz seemed to take an intense dislike to this man and ordered him about with insults and threats.

The schooner's name was covered and sentries placed fore and aft. I was guarding the focs'l.

The plan was to locate the cable and reconnoitre the exact position of the cable office. When darkness fell, the sub would slip into the harbour. As soon as the cable was cut we would flash a green light and the shelling would begin. U694 would then take everyone off the scuttled Blackduck and head to sea. The vessels crew was to be treated as P.O.W.'s.

It was now raining with patchy fog and only a few small boats were seen. One came close by. The schooner Captain, at gunpoint, told him he was a banker out of Harbour Grace looking for squid.

The cable was located with the help of magnets and exact underwater sketches. The diver rested; then just after dark, descended with his cutting tools. The sub had slipped away into the harbour. Only vestiges of twilight remained. Lt. Schultz was guarding the diving apparatus. The young giant was 10 feet away, holding a line. Suddenly he leapt, grabbed Schultz in an instant, lifted him and threw him overboard. He then grabbed the oxygen apparatus and threw it in the sea and, with the same movement, leaped overboard and landed feet first on the struggling Schultz. At the same instant, a shot was fired from the focs'l companionway and seaman Graff fell. I felt pain in my left chest. There must have been a hidden shotgun that we missed. Rapid fire now followed. Three of the Newfoundlanders were killed. Two jumped overboard and were shot in the water, their positions revealed by phosphorescence. The Blackduck was now listing to starboard as the fishermen had opened the seacocks. The diver and Schultz were lost. Graff was dead. I was helped into a dory and we left the sinking schooner. About 20 minutes later, U694, having abandoned the mission when the fighting broke out, picked us up and headed out to sea.

Matt clicked off the recorder. For many seconds there was only the sound of surf. A pebble exploded among the embers.

"Lord sufferin', and to think it all happened just out there."

"Please summarize the rest of his story, would you? We've only heard bits and pieces."

"Well," Matt said, "Cadger claims he was a double agent at that time and was passing information to the British through a girlfriend working at a Turkish restaurant in Hamburg. Says he first made contact with British intelligence while at the German embassy in Dublin in 1940. His code name was Tristan. He had a sudden change from Nazi fervour to the realization that he was part of a monstrous crime against humanity when they sank a ship on a winter night in the North Sea. He lay in a warm bunk knowing innocent lives faced terror and death just yards away.

When he returned to Germany after the Heart's Content episode he became depressed, drank heavily and deserted the Navy. After that, he made his way, with Turkish help, to Kushadasi and from there to Greece, ending up in a small house near Navpaktos. There he drank a lot, became interested in Rationalism and the enigma of human behaviour. After the war, he contacted his brother in Majorca who helped him financially, as there had been an inheritance. He seems to have developed an obsession with Newfoundland and the sea. Later he overcame his addiction to the booze and decided to return to the scene of the crime via sailboat. His defence rests entirely on if, and when, he became a British spy."

The last red lobster claw gave up its succulent flesh.

"Sure now—what's Rationalism?"

"The Oxford dictionary defines Rationalism as the principle of accepting Reason as the supreme authority in matters of belief or conduct."

"Oh, ere's a rational request b'y—hand over the beans."

They sat quietly, smelling wood smoke and feeling the last heat of a summer day, each thinking of the tragedy that had unfolded a few yards away when the struggle between fascism and democracy extended to these quiet shores. Matt remembered when he had first heard of the mystery of the *Blackduck*, in the focs'l of the Winnifred Bea, caught in Arctic ice. He marvelled at the passage of time.

"So what about this Cadger, Matt, hero or villain?"

"Hey, the jury is out on that one."

Venus had followed the sun below the dark hills of Trinity North when they broke camp and motored past the Lousy Rock toward the lights of home.

CHAPTER 41

▼

The trial aroused great interest—a close and loquacious society felt violated by evil from afar. But, as the story unfolded, the frontier between guilt and innocence shifted like sea sand. Cadger refused council. He was a gaunt defendant. His intellect and intensity were apparent. He began by saying he did not know whether he was guilty or not. He then, over several days, described being caught in a torrent of human events—of war, remorse, depression, addictions, of a growing fervour to understand, to explain, of reclaiming his consciousness from the forces that had enslaved and of his finding salvation in the brilliance of the scientific method: the democracy of truth; the fraternity of explanation.

The jury returned after 1½ days of deliberation. Moisture laden air had spun in tight isobars along the Eastern seaboard of North America, fringing a massive, cold continental high. St. John's rocked in a white wind. The Courthouse creaked. The lights flickered. Cars hid in snow banks.

"Order!"

"In the case of Wilhelm Prostner vs. the Queen, we find the defendant, not guilty."

There was subdued handclapping. Matt rushed forward and embraced old Cadger, now suddenly faced with the adjustments to freedom.

"Congrats old timer—hey you're free! I'll call Vanessa. We must have a celebration."

While Cadger was besieged by the press, Matt telephoned Vanessa who was snow-trapped at home and unable to come downtown.

Matt and Cadger leaned on the gale and in a few minutes arrived, snow encrusted, at the Ship Inn, where with many jovial fellow travelers, they toasted the future with hot rum and made plans for old Cadger to stay with the Penwells while considering his options.

CHAPTER 42

▼

Six months later, when September was changing costumes, Matt and Vanessa left Deer Lake and drove northwest on Highway 430 toward Gros Morne National Park. Matt recalled the day he and Jonathan had discovered the skeletal arm on Sealcove Beach. It was on that same day years ago that he had first heard from Jonathan—the fledgling engineer—about neutrinos and antimatter and they had pledged to learn all that there was to know about the Universe and to record this search for truth in book form. Since then they had met a group of like-minded individuals, had become friends, and had combined their love of science and the natural world with discussion-vacations at various destinations in the Great Island. This autumn, their destination was Gros Morne. Vanessa and Matt had just spent two days salmon fishing at Big Falls on the upper Humber River. The van was crammed with camping gear and bicycles. Two sea kayaks were strapped to the roof. They were driving through the southern section of the Long Range Mountains, which form the backbone of the great northern peninsula.

"Cadger's become quite a celebrity."

"Indeed. Radio and T.V. loves him—he's so elegant and passionate. Jonathan told me Wilhelm has been in a manic phase for the last bit though; how sad he has to ride that roller coaster."

"Yes that's a shame. Too bad Rachel couldn't come, I'm told she is at some feminist frolic in Halifax."

"I hear MUN has suggested he write memoirs and be a guest lecturer …"

Their conversation was interrupted by the vista of Bonne Bay—a lucent blue carpet wandering in from the Gulf of St. Lawrence—leading the eye to an upsurge of mountains, with Gros Morne soaring to 806 metres. "Ah, what magnificence. This should be great and the forecast is encouraging."

"Everybody will be here. Jonathan is flying in from Churchill Falls. He's working on a new idea to try and salvage some value for Newfoundland from the debacle of the 70-year give away to Hydro Quebec—something about hydrogen fuel cells."

"And Nigel will fly in tomorrow. He vows now that he will sail across in two years for the session at Heart's Content."

"Great! He'll be able to sail Trinity and Bonavista Bays."

"Tom and the boys are building tourist cabins near the beach that should be available in two years, and there are some good tourist homes nearby."

They had all gathered by Thursday evening. Tents were pitched on a small plateau profuse with wildflowers and set back a few yards from a pebble beach. On the left a brook terminated in the Gulf of St. Lawrence, with the flourish of a twenty foot cascade into a tidal pool. Mature spruce and tamarack marched up the foothills of the Long Range Mountains. The evening was spent around campfires. Everyone had a story and all were enthralled by the natural beauty.

Next morning dawned mild and foggy. They breakfasted and swam in the pool, and then Jonathan herded them all unto the little plateau.

Matt presided.

"I'll begin by introducing our special guest, a man whose dramatic story has merged here with a great sea mystery and has touched us all—Captain Wilhelm Prostner."

Wilhelm rose slowly. He had a fringe of white hair on the back of his head. He walked to the grassy platform, stopping to pick the seed-pod of a wild iris. Blue eyes were bright in an animated face. All was quiet, except for the sounds of the brook.

"Pleased and honoured am I to be a part of this group," he said, "I understand this all began as a long term dream, a pact really, between Matt and Jonathan when they were mere youths, 'To follow knowledge, like a shooting star, beyond the utmost bound of human thought'—ah Tennyson. What a dream indeed. I would suggest a preface to their book that would challenge the individual to enter a marathon of the mind. After all, we spend much of life's energy challenging physical limits, why not an intellectual Everest?" He looked around at the hills and ocean. "This place is like a stern mother who disciplines, then suddenly smiles, and we are enthralled. Such a vast beauty and so few to share it. Shhh. Don't tell anyone!

"My subject is Human Behaviour, an intriguing and enigmatic chameleon indeed! It all begins and ends with biology's greatest accomplishment—the human brain. 10 billion they say, or is it 100 billion neurons? A massive number anyway, like the dollars we give to Quebec." He shook with laughter. "I am laughing with you, not at you, I am one with you! There are many factors that determine how we behave—ve vill simplify, ve vill boil the meat off ze bones like for dinner. Sorry mit der accent—I have been vatching too much *Hogan's Heroes*. Okay, now we are more serious! So why are the Afghanis different from the Swedes? I think we can agree that the programming of the children is the main determinant; that vulnerable defenceless brain, it's future totally dependent on the input it will receive. Oh my, what a responsibility we have! How will the poor little bugger be educated?

"Matt, may I have a coffee? This will change my behaviour too.

"Now, education can either be faith-based or science-based. The nations show a spectrum; most with some combination of both. On one end, we have Theocracies, with Secular Democracies on the other. I have a slide to compare the two." Wilhelm searches in his pockets. "Don't worry—one slide only." Then, after much rummaging, "Drat, I must have forgotten it!" The audience is somewhat amused and restive. "I will make a slide of myself," said Wilhelm, and he stretched out both his arms. "Hey, now I am a Christian symbol! The Theocracies are in my right hand and the Secular Democracies in my left—you can fit all the world's nations in between. Here is Iran," he wiggles his right hand, "and here is say, France. This is just the bones, you get the meat when we get to Heart's Content—hey that sounds like a song!" Wilhelm did a little twirl. "Isn't there a line '*by the time I get to Houston*—never mind, no matter. I will just tell you that a comparison between Theocracies and Democracies gives truly astounding results, with one being a clear winner for Humanity. Actually you only have to read The UN's list of the best countries to live in on this planet.

"You would not let anyone take over your house or car without a great fight. Yet we let people take over our consciousness, our intelligence, not only without protest, but often with obsequious obedience. The great crime is that much of this theft is done when we are innocent children dependent on the quality of sensory input. We allow other people with agendas, isms and especially religions, to capture large portions of our intelligence, which is lying fallow. It appears that this propensity for submission to leaders and ritual was part of a primitive, evolutionary strategy, which at the time, was successful in the survival of more progeny. There are similarities throughout biology: birds, animals, insects, fish, all flock, herd, swarm and school to decrease the chance of individual predation and maximize the benefits of numbers. These tendencies persist in a primitive part of our brains—the reptilian brain—though now entirely inappropriate to modern human society; resulting in the chaos and tragedy we see everywhere today, where human beings, enslaved to religious or cultish superstition, are prepared, nay consider it a duty and privilege, to mutilate and massacre people of other superstitions, in return for promised after-death rewards. The reptilian brain seems everywhere to trump the cerebral cortex. Whatever can be the answer?

"The accumulation of knowledge via the scientific method is the answer. The brilliance of science, of the cerebral cortex, in explaining our universe in a flash of cosmic time is truly astounding. The story is wondrous but can be outlined, highlighted, by 20 or 30 headlines and I suggest a card, bearing the steps to human wisdom be inserted in the cover of this book, giving at a glance, the immense sweep of scientific explanation.

"I am becoming disconnected now," said Wilhelm, rubbing his brow, "I will stop. Thank you again for inviting me to this beautiful place."

"Questions anyone?"

"So what is the practical answer, Wilhelm?" asked Nigel.

"You want the answer? I say the UN should pass a decree that no child can have faith-based programming until age eighteen, but I won't say that because I also forgot my bullet proofed vest."

"But what about the communists, they don't accept the supernatural and they promote scientific education?"

"Ah," answered Wilhelm, "but they are not Democratic; Democracy is everything—freedom is what enhances the quality of everyman's life; dignity, confidence, absence of fear!"

"What about the United States? It is very religious and democratic."

"The U.S.," replied Wilhelm, "It is an enigma, don't ask me why it is one of the most religious nations. But it is still saved from itself by the Constitution that separates Church and State. For how long? Who knows!"

"What about other causes of behaviour like hormones and emotions?" asked Sandy Walton.

"A great battle rages in us all—war between reason and emotion! Generals Testosterone and Estrogen, among others, run the emotional show—love, lust, jealousy, pleasure—the whole structure is riddled with subjectivity and irrationality. Let me quote you a verse from that old communist rascal, Pablo Neruda, which speaks to the ubiquity of the sensual:

The homosexual young men and the amorous girls,
And the lone widows who suffer from delirious insomnia
And the young wives thirty hours pregnant,
And the raucous cats that cross my garden in the dark
Like a necklace of throbbing sexual oysters …
there is a continuous life of trousers and skirts,
a rustle of stroked silk stockings,
And feminine breasts that shine like eyes.

"Mother Nature controls our behaviour for her favourite result: progeny!"

"Yes B'y," said Seth, who was taking Tom's place as caretaker, we're all like dat partridge cock I just saw down the trail, 'e fell down a gully and landed wid a t'ump, 'is feders all in a 'rection, chasin' a female who flew up in a tree. 'E picks 'imself up an starts bein' a damn fool all over agin'."

"That's it," said Jonathan, when the laughter died down. "Thank you, Captain. That was interesting and thought provoking. Actually, Matt has written something similar to the card you suggest—in the form of a poem called, The Rationalist's Creed. I will read some of the poem's opening lines when I talk about the nuts and bolts of the Universe after a break."

They sat and strolled and chatted in the enchantment of the morning, all the while being entertained by the sights and sounds of fishermen unloading and cleaning a midship room full of cod just a few Stages away. Then Jonathan clanged on a frying pan and they reassembled.

"I'll begin with the lines I promised from Matt's poem," he began.

That first big bang
Both time and space began
And energy that cooled to quarks
Which protons plan.

Then atoms—the parent hydrogen.
Hidden within the mix were forces four:
Let's talk of gravity
That in an orchard green
Would speak to Newton …

"We are at the beginning of the universe—the big bang. Before the great explosion, there was no time or space, only a microscopic kernel of infinitely dense mass/energy. This hypothesis is now widely accepted by the scientific community for two main reasons I will talk about later.

"From about one hundredth thousandth of a second after the explosion began, science has a good explanation of what has happened in the intervening 15 billion years—from then to the present instant. The explosion was a seething tempest of radiant energy and particles at unimaginable temperatures—a trillion, trillion degrees. Many exotic particles are produced, each particle having its antiparticle and, if and when the newborn pairs collide, they annihilate each other by turning again into radiant energy. Then protons form from quarks and electrons and neutrons appear. The initial temperatures cool rapidly with the expansion of the universe, and a mere four minutes after the big bang, the mass of the universe consisted of 75% hydrogen nuclei (which is one proton) and 35% helium nuclei—our very first ancestors. Intense radiation made up of all the wavelengths of the electromagnetic spectrum—from gamma waves to radio waves—bombarded the protons, neutrons and electrons, and it was not until 700,000 years after the explosion that radiation cooled enough to allow negative electrons to bind to the positive protons, forming hydrogen and helium atoms."

"Right," said Nigel, waving his right hand across his face. "By the way, the bloody flies are eating me alive! So, 700,000 years after the big bang we have mass in the form of hydrogen and helium, plus radiant energy, which is cooling and losing intensity and changing to mass as the universe expands. The future of radiant energy is somewhat boring as it continues to cool and lose intensity to this day. For hydrogen and helium, however, the future is filled with drama including the formation of life on the beautiful planet Earth. In fact, hydrogen has been called the machine that produced the universe. Sorry Jonathan, I didn't mean to take over."

"Please, anytime, Nigel. This is really a conversation. Sorry, I'm being rather didactic with this bit. By the way, sit in the wood smoke or put on some dope to save good English blood."

"The vast clouds of hydrogen and helium develop fluctuations, or areas of different density, which under the influence of gravity, form great rounded gas masses and contract into the earliest stars. The centers of stars heat up because of gravitational effects causing compression and eventually a giant nuclear furnace is formed. In this furnace, intense heat, pressure and radiant energy create new atoms. These atoms have more protons, neutrons and electrons borrowed from the original hydrogen and helium and we have the elements we know today. These 100 plus elements, including the 15 or so that create human beings, were and are literally created, in the great furnace factories of the stars. We are stardust! Then, some of these stars become supernovas. They overheat, explode, and scatter all the elements into space as gas and dust.

"Now history repeats and these clouds of elements and gases become irregular in density and under the pull of gravity, form great spheres. In this way, our planet and sun were formed. Under gravity, the lighter elements such as silicon and magnesium shift to the surface while heavier elements move toward the core. Intensely hot and heavy iron forms the core of the Earth. The skin of the planet cools and contracts forming a wrinkled rocky crust. Earth's core is not hot enough to have a nuclear furnace, so all the elements—gold, silver, platinum, etc. were born in the stars.

"Now the Earth is held by a noose of gravity in an orbit around our sun. For billions of years it is fiery, radiant, but gradually cooling. The ionized inner core creates magnetic fields, which turn the sphere into a huge magnet. Somebody say a few words while I have some tea."

"Well," said Sandy Walton, "somewhere early on in your book you should emphasize the elegant simplicity underlying the universe. People think only of mind-boggling complexity because that's the way it's taught."

Sandy continued, "Two key concepts: First, everything is either in the form of energy or mass and the two convert into each other via Einstein's lovely formula $E = MC^2$, or energy equals mass times the speed of light squared. All energy is encompassed in the Electromagnetic Spectrum, which consists of wave-particle radiation, or photons, that differ only in wavelength. So you go from the shortest and most powerful gamma ray, to the longest and weakest radio waves, with all the other wavelengths, e.g. ultraviolet, light, infrared, etc. in between.

"Biology evolved organs to detect only a tiny part of this spectrum: eyes to interpret the light wavelength and heat sensors to detect microwaves. Then human brains, through science, invented machines that can detect all the electromagnetic spectrum: radio, radar, T.V., x-rays and so on. This is how science has been able to investigate, to "see" the universe, both large and small.

"Secondly, as you said, all that stuff that was flying about right after the big bang, settled down with cooling and in a few minutes out popped protons, neurons and electrons. The point I'm trying to make is that all matter in the universe, everything we are and see, was built by just adding protons, neutrons and electrons to the original hydrogen and helium atoms. Add four protons and four neutrons to a helium nucleus and you have a carbon nucleus. Simple building blocks, tinker toys, beautifully elegant, if I may repeat myself."

"Great Sandy! An excellent contribution. Ok, we've covered a few billion years. Let's have lunch."

They lunched on potato salad, squid and snow crab.

"Hey," said Matt. "I suggest we put a reef in this next session. It looks like a fine afternoon, summer sou'west wind and a quiet sea. Some people might want to jig for cod in the bay or fly-fish in the river. We could boil up later on the beach. What do you say, Vanessa?"

"I'm still thrilling from my 15 minute contest with a salmon at Big Falls. I want to do and see everything in this place. So get on with it Matthew!"

"Here we go. By the way, I neglected to welcome Professors Walker from Southampton University, Moore from Oberlin and Veenis from Nipissing. We hope you enjoy yourselves and come back with friends in two years time."

"So we now know the origin of our dear Earth. This may well be the luckiest of all planets because it gradually cooled to a surface temperature that allows water to exist in all three states: liquid, solid and gas. Hydrogen and oxygen combine inside the earth, form H20, which passes to the surface and mingles with other gases—carbon dioxide, methane, hydrogen sulphide etcetera—to form an atmosphere, which is kept in place by Earth's gravity—all such a delicate balance.

"Now, in this exotic place, the scene is set—water, carbon dioxide, methane, radiant energy from our star and from lightning—now something wonderful is about to happen. Hot oceans and ponds full of these and other simple substances are stirred for millions of years by radiant energy. Life is an event waiting to happen."

"Matt," Nigel said, "as you know, we can produce complex molecules in the laboratory, even the precursors of proteins and DNA itself, by mimicking the conditions of early earth. Also remember that when complex organic molecules formed in the ancient seas they were alone on stage. There was no predation and no oxidation. These compounds would quickly be destroyed today by other beasties and by oxygen."

"Good points, Nigel, and remember these compounds were floating in the organic soup with 'hands' stretched out, as it were, trying to attach to other molecules. These 'hands' mean the presence of positive or negative electrochemical charges on a molecule, which comes about when an electron is lost or gained, producing ions. The objective in chemical reactions is to achieve electrical neutrality. Electromagnetic processes are the basis of all biochemistry and therefore of all life. The Earth was a molecular Garden of Eden with all the energies of the electromagnetic spectrum crashing in from the sun, knocking electrons off molecules and thereby creating ions. Imagine a molecule moving about with four electromagnetic hands outstretched. Organic fragments that 'fit' electromagnetically grasp these hands. Now you have two identical molecules attached and if they break apart, say by radiant energy impact, you have two identical separate molecules both with outstretched electromagnetic receptors. You have replication—you have life! Very soon, these replicating molecules would dominate the sea and minor changes brought about by radiant energy impact—gamma rays mostly—would alter the compounds. Now the building blocks of proteins appear, and purines and pyrimidines, the building blocks for the master planner itself—DNA. We have life!

"These organic molecules grew to great size by adding more and more attachments. They grow into blue green algae which cover and fill the oceans and ponds for 3 billion years."

"And remember," Professor Veenis commented, "these blue green algae produced molecular oxygen which gradually became a significant part of the Earth's atmosphere. Oxygen was toxic and destroyed many organic compounds in the soup. Others survived by adaptation, so in a sense oxygen stimulated the whole process. We have some amazing organisms, which adapted to the oxygen toxicity and still survive as tetanus and botulism bacteria, their metabolism functions without oxygen—they are anaerobes."

"Thanks Marie Françoise, for introducing that magic word, 'adaptation'. That's enough for now; let's break off early. Any questions?"

"Just a comment really," Prostner answered. "My main input will come when we discuss the psyche of homo sapiens, but I think all this becomes more believable if one sits quietly and considers the enormous time frame of these events, the number of chances, the immense number of failures before the stage is set for a tiny advance. Billions of years with trillions of chances every millionth of a second you might say."

"Ok, we'll break early and re-assemble in the morning."

*   *   *   *

Squid for bait.
Life struggling to escape, pulled from the depths.
Cod.
Vanessa despairs, but partakes at dinner.
Trout rising to the fly.
Keels grounding on pebbles.
The view from headlands.
Whale majesty.
Blackflies.
Summer evening solace.
Campfires.
Sunset colours of sea and sky.
The nostalgia of connections.
"Let me fish off Cape St. Mary's"
Outport lights.
Conversation.
Embers.
Sleep.
Morning. Sounds of surf and seagulls.

"Now me sons," said Jonathan, lapsing into the vernacular, "tis a different day for sure. You can smell the rain. I'll guarantee you she'll blow before dark. My dear she can blow here! B'y, I says if dat Newton fellar was sittin' under an apple tree in dis country, 'e never would 'ave discovered gravity because apples 'ere usually flies horizontal when dey lets go of the tree. Anyway, let's begin as it won't hit for a few hours."

Vanessa was Chairwoman.

"First, are there any comments on yesterday's session?"

"Matt promised yesterday that he would discuss the reasons why the scientific community accepts the 'Big Bang' theory," said Professor Moore.

"Matt, will you speak to that please?"

"Oh yes. Two major predictions stemmed from the Big Bang theory and amazingly, they have both been proven true. First, Edwin Hubble found that the spectra of all distant galaxies are red shifted, which means they are all moving away from us, and the farthest galaxies move the fastest. This means that the universe is still flying apart. Reverse the video and it would come together. Hubble, of course, used the Doppler effect. Like sound, the wavelength of light decreases slightly as it comes toward us and its spectral lines are blue shifted—it's a blue light. Going away from us, wavelengths are slightly increased and red shifted.

"Secondly, it was predicted that the background radiant energy—which we earlier said had a boring future, that is, it would gradually cool and lose intensity as the universe expanded—should still be detectable in the universe. This is a great story. Two chaps were listening for radio waves from different parts of the cosmos. They kept hearing a faint buzz, which they thought was due to pigeon droppings on the antenna. Anyway, subsequently, it was proven by satellite antenna, that there is faint uniform radio transmission coming from all parts of the cosmos at just the temperature and intensity predicted mathematically for this point in time. These two amazing proofs have convinced just about all the scientific community.

"Thanks," said Vanessa. "Let's get on with it before we have to batten down. Yesterday we went from the Bang to Blue Green Algae. From here, wonderful things happen. 600 million years ago the algae empire was broken in what we know as the Cambrian explosion of life. Many new forms appear. 500 million years ago, strange insect-like creatures roamed in packs, the trilobites. New variations appear, wax and wane, disappear or dominate. We can't detail it here, of course. In the great lottery of chance, the winning adaptations produced fish, amphibians, vertebrates, insects and flight, trees, reptiles, dinosaurs, mammals, dolphins, primates—and man.

"Now I will focus on two immense origins, two brilliant concepts of the large human brain on which our understanding advances. Let me quote a paragraph from '*The Selfish Gene*', by Richard Dawkins: '*Intelligent life on a planet comes of age when it first works out the reason for its own existence. If superior creatures ever visit Earth, the first question they will ask, in order to assess the level of our civilization is, "Have you discovered evolution yet?"*'

"Living organisms had existed on Earth, without ever knowing why, for over 3 billion years before the truth finally dawned on one of them. His name was Charles Darwin.

"Darwin's conclusions, based upon the observations and detailed species' studies during the *Voyage of the Beagle*, were at once so simple that contemporaries said, 'Why didn't I think of that?' and at the same time so all powerful and ubiquitous in their application that it has taken over a hundred years for philosophy, the humanities, even zoology, to come to grips with the immensity of the implications."

"No mathematical formulas," said Dr. Bonfield, "just adaptation by natural selection and the survival of the fittest. Think about it! This provides the framework for understanding what happened from the atomic-molecular dance in soupy seas to the phenomenon of Human Consciousness."

"Any questions?"

There was only silence. A gust of wind caused the campfire embers to burst into flames.

"The second achievement, which fitted hand and glove into Darwin's concepts, was the discovery of the master planner of all biology—the secret living blueprint of all life—the double helix—Deoxyribonucleic acid (DNA)! The story of this breakthrough by Watson and Crick is human and dramatic.

"Now, let's jump back into the primitive soup. We know that energy striking simple organic compounds can produce purines and pyrimidines in the laboratory setting. These are the building blocks of

DNA, which consists of two very long chains twisted around each other, each containing a sequence of four nucleic acids, adenine, thymine, cytosine and guanine. (A.T.C.G.)—four outstretched hands. A separate blueprint of DNA is present in every one of our bodies' thousand million million cells. All animals and plants have identical DNA to ours, except that the sequence of A.T.C.G. is changed. DNA is immortal. DNA replicates itself by splitting the spiral staircase in half and then latching on to identical amino acids with electromagnetic 'hands' as in our 'chemical' sea. DNA is the masterpiece, which via the complex mechanisms of biochemistry, is responsible for all the characteristics of every individual and species on Planet Earth.

"DNA is very stable. However, changes can occur; possibly a random strike by a gamma ray from Mother sun may result in changes in offspring. This may be lethal and cause death, or it may cause a change in the host allowing it to adapt better to its environment and increase the chance of survival. From this source comes the variety and complexity of biology. In this we see how close we are to fellow mortals and fellow species."

"How marvellous," said Professor Moore. "We need to create other words in the language to adequately depict such beauty."

"One must remind oneself," said Vanessa, trying to control her long hair in the wind, "that DNA has no purpose, no brain, that all the complexity of life forms is the result of random chance and the physical-chemical forces described."

"Now the storm comes and Jonathan is motioning me to stop. May I add that if anyone wishes to write a poem or essay on any of these things, we would be delighted. As we close, I will continue the reading of, *'The Rationalists' Creed'*:

> *... It herded molecules into great balls*
> *Infernos punctuate with celestial fires,*
> *There, in nuclear cores,*
> *New atoms breed*

And when these stars
By little big bangs torn
Are spread through space
Then debris isles are formed,
Of which our Earth was one.
Adorned with gifts from space
She orbits 3rd rock from the mother sun.
Now, stroked by time
The elements did brood
In soupy seas and river mud,
Stirred and enhanced
By input from old sol.
What's this!—new molecules!
What! Now they split in two!
Electrified—biology begins,
Adapts
And sends the fittest down the road
That 'neath an English sky
Would lead to Darwin …

"See you in two years. Bring friends! We will consider the human psyche. Has the human brain outstripped the determinism of DNA; escaped the constraints of evolution? What is the nature of consciousness? Good-bye."

Then there was conversation and laughter amid the rising sounds of wind and surf. Flames flared yellow below the blackened pot. A green black lobster in the predator's hand paused above the boil, a flash of sorrow in the torturer's eye and then the lid descends. Now, appetite, sans remorse, besieges red-shelled bodies.

Dark scudding clouds.

Spray on the wind.

Bakeapple jam.

Stand by the sea and scream euphoria to the gale.
Lie, snug in your sleeping bag, warm, listening …

Vanessa's voice. Vanessa, sitting on a log, sipping vodka from icebergs 10,000 years old, a high happy voice above the wind.

"I must read you this from the great Sagan: '*There are tens of billions of known kinds of organic molecules. Yet only about fifty of them are used for the essential activities of life. The same patterns are employed over and over again, conservatively, ingeniously for different functions. At the very heart of life on Earth. The proteins that control cell chemistry and the nucleic acids that carry hereditary instructions. We find these molecules to be essentially identical in all plants and animals.*'

"Flowers and I are made of the same stuff," she shouted. "The lobster is us … and you should hear what he says about trees …" but the gale blew louder and her voice was lost, and then again in a lull, "And here's the ending to Matt's poem."

> *… From fire to sentience,*
> *From quarks to consciousness,*
> *From rote to reason in the human brain,*
> *We who now hold the torch*
> *Upon the spear of time*
> *We winners now should brothers be,*
> *And cherish all!*

They broke camp the next morning vowing to meet again in two years at Heart's Content.

CHAPTER 43

▼

Jonathan, yes b'y!

Today I climbed th' mizzen hill and walked around Daniel's pond lookin' for a crooked cedar for a stemhead—me b'ys plan on building a long liner next winter. Th' sun was warm on me face, ice is 'alf gone from th' ponds, you can 'ear it grumble as it melts along th' shore. Mud trout will be anxious for flies and th' German browns t'inkin' about goin' down to d'sea. Some drift ice still in th' bay but th' seals 'ave mostly all taken to th' water.

Lots of stuff on T.V., b'y. Jonathan, I gotta admit I've taken a real shine to th' Monica Lewinski woman, she looks some nice! I says to myself, 'my son dat would be like fresh squid on a white plate. Oh my!'

Now you're some lucky to be 'earin' from me 'cause I near drowned. Joshua saved me for sure and he only 9 years old! I untied th' boat, shoved 'er off, pulled on th' outboard and, somehow she started in gear at high revs. She took off for deep gulch and I took off over th' engine into th' harbour. I can't swim, no life jacket, rubber boots on! She goes around in a tight circle, hits me and sends me down. I'm drownin'! My son, I was some scared. Joshua climbs back aft and stops th' engine. Then he sculls her over to me. I been down four times—never mind, t'ree. Joshua grabs hold of me, den another fellar dives in and dey gets me to shore. Dey bailed me out in hospital for two days.

Anyway, I'm fine. Dey say St. Peter gives Newfoundlanders a room near th' door 'cause he knows dey'll want to go home in a week or so, so I would 'ave come back!

Sorry I didn't get to th' shindig at Gros Morne—we were huntin and fishin from our cabin on Gander River. I enjoy all dat talk. It gets you t'inkin' but sometimes when I get d'ere I'm only 'alfway. We'll be ready for you when you come 'ere—sure 'tis only a few months away! We'll 'ave fun.

B'y I can't tell you how nice th' harbour looks right now, it can sure quieten your brain. Moose stew for supper.

All th' best,

Tom

CHAPTER 44

───────────── ▼ ─────────────

Almost two years later, the brave sloop *Lorna Doone* stood in for St. John's harbour as the sun's first rays reached North America on August 16th. Captain Nigel and his Cambridge associate, Jeremy Magras, had departed Fowey, in Devon, on June 14th and circled north to the Faeroes, through misty seas to Iceland, then S.W. on the East Greenland current to Cape Farewell, from where—aided by the Labrador drift—they sailed almost due south for St. John's. Their faces were bronzed and bearded, their consciousness awed and elated by the implacable and tempestuous beauty of the North Atlantic.

The harbour dawned like a smile on the face of great cliffs that roamed north and south of the narrow entrance. In an hour, they were tied up just below the distinguished memorial to those who died in the wars of the British Empire.

Matt and Jonathan were at dockside and, after the sailors showered, the four made their way along Water Street for a pub lunch. They yarned over beer and pan-fried cod.

"I'm amazed," said Jeremy. "How can there be such a marvellous place lying unknown and undeveloped half-way between London and New York? Tell us something about your history, please."

"Yes, actually we are a little south of London, but we lost the Atlantic currents lottery—you bathe in the Gulf Stream while the

Arctic current chills our shores. Also, the currents meet S.E. of here so we get the world's best fog thrown in."

"As far as history goes," said Jonathan, "we, the first overseas colony, have been ready to serve the British Empire from square one, and quite a colourful and bloody role it has been. We actually were the senior Dominion, but we went bankrupt in the crash of the thirties, and then, it seems, you Brits dealt us into Canada without first giving us back self-government, as you had promised."

"Ouch!" said Nigel.

"Oh, I'm sure you thought you were doing us a big favour."

"And were we?"

"Well, our once marvellous fishery has collapsed. The outports are dying. Our young people must leave by the thousands. Canada gets all the profits from the Great Labrador Hydro development. We are broke. They keep us afloat on socialist handouts."

"Sounds like you've traded British colonial status for Canadian."

"That about sums it up. We look at Iceland and the Faeroes and feel that we've missed a few boats along the way."

"'We moored ourselves alongside the wrong wharf', as the old fellow said."

"Oh come on, lighten up!" said Nigel, laughing. "After all, we gave you language, freedom, literature, democracy, science, and games even, and you do seem quite a resolute, happy lot. So just sort it out and get it right."

A customer of uncertain age with long grey hair and a flowing beard has been drinking and listening. Now he turns to Nigel and speaks, his face darkly mysterious in silhouette against the light from the street. He is well-spoken with a sonorous voice, low and soft like the first whispers of an approaching gale.

"This is an island, beautiful and bold, set in cross currents of the northern sea. Here was a plenitude of fish and foul and game. The seas, now as always, laden with a plankton feast, a soup to start the food chain. The land, tundra and barrens, mountains and rivers, resplendent in seasonal garb, present a visage harsh that disciplines, but often smiles.

"Now spice with homo sapiens: First Inuit, a sprinkle of fated Beothuk, a touch of Viking, then—in devilish mood—English and Irish, drawn from quarrels old. But nature scraped the quarrels from their bones and, for survival's sake, the dissonance of man-created enmity subsides, leaving a peaceful Isle, plus Labrador, where man lives close to nature—nature stern to discipline—but with beauty to entrance.

"The Island casts a spell, a challenge to survive along a harsh and lovely shore. They seek the fish—the cod—and spread with generation's wave to coves and inlets, tickles and bays along 10,000 miles. Resourceful, independent and self-reliant, they had no help from governments. The sea claimed yearly tolls, as did disease, but they held fast.

"Colony, Dominion free, colony again. Now, fateful choice—Confederate or free? Maybe the Gods do punish those who sell their souls for potage: We killed the thing we loved!"

Nigel raised his hand, but the old man slammed his fist on the table and continued.

"But hold! It seems that London dealt the cards with Ottawa that sealed our fate. Now fifty years have passed. We are last by every measure and ridiculed! Wealth: hydro, minerals, oil—good capital that could create work and initiatives flows to the mainland and bad capital, in the form of socialist programs, arrives in brown envelopes in the mailbox.

"Where we traded with many countries we are now blocked from markets. We sell our hydro at the border for no profit while Quebec makes a billion annually. Our children migrate but the unemployment rate is still 20%. Our outports wither."

His voice flowed with a passionate sadness.

"What can be done? Wither this lethargy, this docility? Do we lack the energy, the critical talent, mass and passion to help ourselves? Where is the old romance that saw us steadfast on land and sea? In the name of our fathers, is there no one who will rally to save this wonderful, beautiful place?"

He sat down. The pub was silent. A foghorn moaned. Then a shout and the patrons rose as one and sang, '*The Ode to Newfoundland*'.

"Well," said Jeremy, in the emotional aftermath, "It appears one should think twice before asking a question around here."

CHAPTER 45

▼

The dark blue Chevy drove away trailing a cloud of dust and with Betty's hand waving through the driver's window. Rachel and Vanessa walked back to the beach where blanket and chairs nestled before a sand dune.

"My stars," said Rachel, "life really does have phases. I could no more manage those two boys now than fly to the moon. Twins, really! Don't know how I raised three, and it was very different then."

"Betty has maternity leave for three months—I think she'll be glad to get back to work."

They looked across the fine dark sand to the surrounding cliffs and the shimmering bay.

"Used to come here for picnics once a summer after we moved to Heart's Content," said Rachel, "we would meet the Bay de Verde branch of the family. I mostly remember fly bites and goose pimples and Uncle Allen from Boston wearing white shoes and roasting salt tomcods wrapped in newspaper on the wood embers."

"Let's have a walk," Vanessa suggested. "There's a path just north of the beach called The Trail of the Eagles."

They walked through beach peas and masses of wild roses and ascended a stepped pathway toward the north headland. The walk was a splendour of sea views and craggy coast. The trail led through black spruce and yellow birch—each tree stamped with its personal epic of survival. The ground underfoot was soft with mosses and decorated with berry blossoms. In a little while, they came to a plateau above a high cliff and sat on the soft, living carpet entranced by the scene before them.

Vanessa broke the silence. "Oh! Congratulations on starting your master's degree. That's great."

"Can you believe it? I can't. A 59-year-old Granny. I can't say how much I enjoy it or how fortunate I feel. Getting my matriculation and then doing University courses has just opened up my little world. Learning sure is expansive; so thrilling and you meet so many great people each of whom is another rocket boost to one's imagination. It's like coming out of a cave unto a teeming floodlit plateau!"

"And then there's Captain Cadger," probed Vanessa.

"Oh! Now it's Wilhelm Prostner since the trial. He has taught me so much. Tom and Sarah haven't met him yet; can't get him to Heart's Content. Says he will come when the group meets there in a couple of years. What an intense, interesting man. Strictly friendship of course." Rachel said with a glance, "He's really still getting over the trial and has many demons from the past. He's brilliant, I think. His main focus now is the effects of religious beliefs on the history of Man—ah Humankind. He's searching for explanation of the extremes of human behaviour—cause and antidote. The University is quite interested and the press still follows him of course. Sorry, I am running on. How unlike me!"

"What is your master's thesis?"

"Distance education. The University is keen on a new project called telemedicine—which is the brainchild of Dr. Rouse. So they are gearing up, and Distance Education is also a natural for our 10,000 mails of coastline. If I do well, I am sure there will be a role for me."

"That's wonderful!" Vanessa said. "We are all so proud of you."

"Things are going well. Roseanne has her bee-hive business and Tom, of course, makes a good living from the sea."

Later they swam where warm river water buffered the frigid sea.

Lying in bed that night, Vanessa still thrilled to the beauty of their day at the beach, and the thought of being surrounded by 8,000 miles of variations on that theme. When Matt was called away to the coronary unit at 3:00 a.m. she went to the kitchen, made a hot chocolate, and wrote:

SALMON COVE

TRAIL OF THE EAGLES

Great cliffs and islands
With fetlocks of foam
Tight tickles and crannies
That eagles call home.
Now lie on moss carpets
And gaze at the sky
To mist shrouded distance
Where schooners sail by.
Oh listen—a moist breath
From out on the Bay
And a plume brightly glowing
Where huge humpbacks play.
This place gives a reason
A recompense too:—
A childhood unending
Where consciousness grew.

CHAPTER 46

▼

The brook fell and foamed, pooled and eddied until it reached the first shore dunes, where it delivered summer warm water, in a long curving glide, to the sea's tidal embrace. Fine black sand, unusual on these pebbled shores, swept the full length of the cove, bound at each end by a spectacular display of eroded rocks that soared red up the sea cliffs. Rocks also rose like dark monuments from the sea with foaming feet where mussels and snails shared the tide with starfish and oozy eggs. The cove provided only poor shelter from Conception Bay, but settled weather had prevailed and the sea shimmered with only a slight swell. Two kayaks lay near the brook and an elegant sloop, flying the Red Ensign, rode quietly to anchor 200 feet offshore.

They lunched on kippers, potato salad, mussels gathered by the kayakers, blueberry duff and tea.

"Have you heard the latest re our friend, Cadger?" asked Jonathan

"No."

"Well, let me get all the names straight first: Wilhelm Prostner is his real name. Donald Cadger, as we call him, is actually his German spy code name. Tristan, he says, was the code name given him by the British when he became a double agent. Documents just released by the British reveal that indeed they had a spy code named Tristan, but he was Maltese and worked out of the British Embassy in Lisbon and was found shot to death in Casablanca in 1944. So, there is no collaboration of the Captain's story there."

"Oh really?"

"Just as well that didn't come out before the trial."

"Well, we'll never know what really happened. I suspect. Cadger himself said he didn't know if he were guilty or not. One way or another, he's paid the price, I think."

"As you know, he's given a $10,000 bursary to help educate descendents of the men who were lost on the *Blackduck*."

"Yes, and when he dies, the *Cormorant* is willed to Burin. He's really well-regarded by most people—popular, even."

They watched as Jeremy Magras rowed ashore in the dinghy, pulled her well up the sand and walked over. "Great Zeus that water is cold," he exclaimed, drying his feet. "I'm sure one would lose various parts of one's anatomy immediately upon immersion!" He had a scar that pulled down the left side of his mouth, which seemed to smile on one side and frown on the other.

"Sit down Jeremy and have a beer. Understand you are a friend of Nigel's. Came all the way from Dublin now didn't you b'y?"

"Actually a hamlet in the south west of Ireland, where the sea cuffs us with wind and mist—much like here I expect, although it's smilin' to-day. Hah, I think I'm still at home what with the surnames and accents! Not easy to get here, you people need your own airline."

"So you are bringing the latest word in physiology. I thought Nigel said psychology—never mind, psychologists are seeing the physiological light these days."

They listened to the quiet, lounging.

"Now Jeremy," said Matt, "it's all about the brain and consciousness to-morrow. Could you give us a thumb nail sketch of the physiological backdrop to this?"

"Sure my friends, honoured I'd be. By the way, this whole project I find fascinating. Poor old Humanity could sure use a dose of rationalism. Anytime superstition has been swept under the mat and knowledge mixed with freedom the Human condition has flourished like wildflowers in July!

"To start a discussion on the brain," Jeremy began slowly, "you must first draw your audience away from the commonplace, have them slip the fetters of the everyday and begin to imagine the magnificence of the organ within the bony helmet of our skulls. We need celestial metaphors: Imagine a clear night sky—10,000 stars are visible—amazing—now multiply that by 100,000 and imagine all these 'lights' were inside your head. That would be a representation of the 10 billion neurons in each of our brains. Now try to visualize each of these neurons having 20 to 50 connections to each other and you have a clue about the immensity and magnificence of the neural web on which our consciousness plays itself out—each neuron or tiny battery that contributes to the electrified web, which sizzles with knowing. We, our awareness, our consciousness, are the ultimate achievement of the Big Bang. All other organs in our bodies are servants striving to create and stabilize the physiological environment in which our brains can function ... and the brain can only function within narrow physiological limits—small changes in ph, in temperature, in glucose or oxygen concentrations, to use a few examples, can quickly change the higher functions of consciousness, of thought and behaviour, and lead to impaired cognition, coma and death."

There was silence except for gulls and the surf. Jeremy was looking down the beach.

"What's happening there?" he asked, pointing to a flurry of gulls and a shining disturbance of water at sand's edge.

"Hey, looks like a capelin spawn to me," said Matt.

They walked over and watched as a cloud of dorsal darkness rolled up on the beach at wave's edge. Bellies flashed as thousands of small fish rolled in a spawning ritual.

"I guess that explains the large number of whales and seabirds we've seen lately. Might as well get a few of these for appetizers later." Jonathan picked up a handful of the shiny fish. "They fit just nicely on your plate."

"Does the physiologist wish to continue?"

"Ah, no. I was actually going for a hike. Luckily the capelin interrupted as I can get quite carried away."

"Right then—thanks. You've set the stage for the weekend."

They watched the Irishman stride away and disappear among the wild roses and balsam that fringed the dunes.

CHAPTER 47

▼

Tom began, "Welcome b'ys to Heart's Content. Sure we've been lookin' forward to dis and d'ere be beds and food enough for all. 'Tis only home where you'd be as welcome as you are' ere! Now you saw th' sands two days ago drivin around th' belt. Yesterday, you looked seaward from Flambro Head, saw th' bird sanctuary on Baccalieu Island and th' lively fishing port of Bay de Verde. Now, me sons, you come to th' great Bay of Trinity—60 miles deep and 15 miles wide, running south west from th' North Atlantic. Nigel and Jeremy saw it th' proper way from th' sea and *Lorna Doone* 'ad a good passage, yes b'y.

"Heart's Content harbour is not as tourist pretty as some; it's a robust, big, working harbour dat can handle any ship. The Great Eastern dropped her hook dere", said Tom, pointing, "built by Isambard Kingdom Brunel—692 feet long, she arrived, the World's biggest ship, reeling out cable all th' way from Ireland, on a foggy July 27th morning in 1866. Anyway, you can learn all about dat at th' museum. Sure b'y, 'tis a nice place. When I gets tormented, I comes 'ere and watches how th' land and sea are gettin along with each other. Seems to put a measure on evert'ing else.

Dat's enough jawing from me. I 'ave a few things to do and I wants to listen too. D'ere'll be lots of talk and plenty to do for sure.

Oh, and if th' weather turns bad, we can all move into th' old cable station."

"Thanks Tom," said Jonathan. "I'd like to quote James Mullahy, who wrote in the New York Herald in 1866, *'All who have visited Trinity Bay, with one consent allow it to be one of the most beautiful sheets of water they ever set eyes upon. Its colour is very peculiar—an inexpressible mingling of the pure blue ocean with the deep evergreen woodlands and the serene blue sky ... '* Heart's Content was an excited place that day and, for a time, the centre of the world. Queen Victoria and President Andrew Jackson exchanged greetings. Heart's Content became the first house of the Global Village."

Matt stood up and put his coffee down in the stern sheets of an old boat that had been stranded for years on the grass of the foreshore. His back was to the harbour. Over the heads of his friends he saw the summit of the Mizzen hill.

"Good morning, friends. This is it! Today it is the brain and consciousness! Jeremy thrilled us at Salmon Cove with an eloquent brief on the complexity, the delicacy and the physiological underpinnings of that magnificent organ. Consciousness is the awareness you have as you sit here. It is unique to you, but connects you to the world of animate and inanimate things. It is a product of the brain. It is a constant play and replay of all the sensory images that have arrived in and been stored, remembered, by your brain.

"The energy that ignites consciousness in our brains is the same type of energy that conveyed the first Morse code message across the Atlantic via the cable in 1866. It is the same energy that fires the Internet today. In fact, one might say that the glow of communications that pervades the earth and surrounding universe—a product of man's intelligence—has given planet earth a form of rudimentary brain, dare we say the beginnings of a planetary consciousness. This energy is purely and simply a flow of electrons.

"Consciousness is everything. Without it, there really is no sound in the forest, no morning light, or perfume from the rose. We are, each of us, privileged to have this conscious space where no one can trespass completely, but at the same time to be connected in a giant horizontal web of the senses, with other people and species.

"Our old friend the electron is front and center in consciousness. You could say the electron is the wave-particle of consciousness, as the photon is the wave particle of electromagnetism. Data arrives in the brain only as electricity, which I will call electron packets. The eyes change light energy to electron packets. The ears change sound wave energy to electron packets, and so on for all the sense organs. No exceptions. The final pathway for all data from outside the brain is the flow, along nerves, of electron packets to the appropriate part of the brain."

"So, you're saying our electrified neural webs are programmed like a computer?"

"Very similar, indeed, except that our 'computer' is so much more sophisticated than any machine we can imagine. Sensory stimuli begin to arrive in utero in what will be a lifelong torrent of data—different, of course, in each individual. It's important to understand that each sensory stimulus produces a different electron package through changes in intensity, or strength of the impulse, and in the 3 dimensional shape of the electromagnetic field that surrounds all electrons. In other words, there is a specific unique electron package for each sensory stimulus that arises from ears, eyes, nose, taste buds—from heat, cold, pain and stretch receptors. This really is an incredible monitoring process that informs the brain of everything and anything that is happening in the body's external and internal environment. At first rudimentary and related to the bare survival needs of the new individual, it progresses rapidly to the astounding sophistication of maturity."

"So," said Nigel, "the eyes don't really see anything, they just change light energy, that has reflected off an object, to electricity (electron packets), and that electrical representation of the object passes along the optic nerve to the appropriate part of the cerebral cortex—the visual cortex in this case, where through some process in the neural net, seeing actually occurs. Is that correct?"

"Yes, and the same process applies to each and every sensory input. In early childhood, your mother repeats names of objects over and over to you, while holding the object before you. Now you have an association between sound and sight. With repetition, the brain learns that the sound 'dog' goes with the visual picture and vice versa and this is stored in memory. The giant leap forward of Homo sapiens compared with the primates was the evolution of a massive cerebral cortex, much of which was dedicated to memory."

"Then, language plays a vital role in consciousness?" asked Vanessa.

"Indeed. It sophisticates consciousness. So-called, 'higher consciousness' likely depends entirely on language. It doesn't matter what language evolves, it's just the learned association of a sound and an object, or with maturity, a concept. There are 1000 words for dog on this planet. The brain just has to be trained. The grasp of language is all-important. We think in terms of names; hence, the vital role of education. The brain is vulnerable."

"Right," said Jeremy. "I'm getting a cup of tea. Now where do you go from here?"

"A little anatomy now. These cortical areas that accept sensory input have wonderful connections, called nerve pathways, with memory storage and with all other parts of the brain. Constant communication occurs with older parts—the mid-brain—where neural structures play a role that was necessary way back on our evolutionary trail. Connections also with basic nuclei in the medulla that control automatic functions such as breathing and to some extent, the heart beat—connections to areas in the frontal lobes that interpret certain electron packets as pleasure or sadness."

"So, its neural net, electron packet, programming, language, memory, intrabrain communication … is this consciousness? How do you define consciousness?"

"Aye, there's a question. In medicine, we know what we mean when we say someone is conscious. It means they are reacting. We also use reflex activity to measure levels of unconsciousness. Dividing the spectrum of biological reaction into reflex, emotional and intellectual consciousness works for me, as it encompasses all life from the reflex activity of the amoeba, to the intellectual achievement of a Nobel Laureate. One must always emphasize, of course, that in the higher animals, all three levels are amazingly intertwined. That's an attempt at classification, the simple definition is that consciousness is awareness."

"But what controls all this awareness that comes with the electron packet-trained brain?"

"Oh, oh," said Tom, "Eye's been runnin' away wi' the line but I t'ink you're goin' to bring him up short now."

"I need some of Jeremy's tea," said Matt, "Nigel, would you like to speak to that?"

"Ah, indeed. Giving me the hottest potato are you? Well, this is important. The leadership of our awareness, the director of consciousness, is a Darwinian phenomenon. It is the strongest electron packet at any one moment. The sequence is the input of a strong stimulus and the associative retrieval of related images from memory. The brain remembers images in order, in categories, in its memory, just like books in a library. When a dominant electron packet arrives in memory, it retrieves a cloud of associated images, like a bullet impacting the desert raises a cloud of sand."

"That's extremely important for understanding consciousness," said Matt, "I repeat, the brain stores electron packet information in association, in related groups, in categories like a library that is built up over time. Then retrieves these related images. For example, say you are sitting by a lake and you hear a loon call. First, you thrill to the beauty of the sound, and then you remember a childhood holiday at a lake where your friend tried to swim too far and had to be rescued. You "see" the evening campfires and "hear" the singing—all in a cascade of associated memory retrieval. Think of your own conscious awareness in an average day; it's a succession of changing dominant electron packets related to external sensory input and associated memory retrieval."

"You make it sound rather simple and almost automatic, rather deterministic," observed Jeremy.

"In essence it likely is rather simple," replied Matt. "Biology has a way of finding something that works and then using it over and over again to create what looks like complexity. To quote Sagan, 'Modern physics and chemistry have reduced the complexity of the sensible world to an astonishing simplicity: Three units (protons, neutrons, electrons) put together in various patterns, make essentially everything.' And to quote from Vanessa's light verse—

> ... *of all the lovely elements*
> *The butterfly takes ten*
> *You only add just 2 or 3*
> *And then you get to men ...* "

"Lard tunderin'," exclaimed Tom, pointing, "Look at Joshua!"

Coming up a small swale, through the sea grass and wild iris, was the 10 year old, tousled, fly bitten and carrying a very large fish.

"Pops," he yelled, "I caught 'im off the wharf. I was fishin' for sculpins and he took the bait."

"My son," Tom exclaimed, "sure dat's a salmon! My what a fine salmon! Sure, Joshua, if those government fellars sees dat, dey'll put you in jail so long you're hair will be whiter than mine. You can't keep 'im, sure."

"'E's almost dead Pop!"

"Well," said Tom, "'e'll taste even better b'y seein' as 'es illegal. Cover 'im up Joshua. 'Ere b'y."

Tom took the salmon and put the silver fish head first down in his rubber boot, covered the top half of the fish with his pant leg and the group watched as 'Pop' and Joshua walked towards home. Joshua gambolling and Tom attempting to show a normal gait.

They broke for lunch on that note—ham sandwiches, speckled trout and partridgeberry pie. Then some people loafed while others walked around the village.

"What about thought?" asked Professor Walton, after they reassembled, "and new ideas? What directs that aspect of consciousness?"

"Thinking is a learned process that requires training," said Vanessa while applying fly dope. "It's a matter of focusing, of concentrating on a subject, of excluding other 'electron packets' from redirecting your consciousness. Original thought? It's a rare phenomenon for sure. Most of us will never have one. Some people say quantum phenomenon may produce original ideas. Hey Matt, is quantum physics involved in consciousness?"

"Nigel, would you give us a short answer to that?" asked Matt.

"All physics is divided into three parts: One, the physics of the very large, Einstein's relativity. Two, the physics of the everyday, which is most acceptable to our logic, Newtonian or classical physics, and three, the physics of the very small—subatomic—called Quantum Mechanics. All three aspects of physics are involved in consciousness: certainly quantum mechanics because it is the realm of the electron.

"Some concepts of quantum physics seem to be beyond the veil of human logic. For example, entanglement of particles, the uncertainty principle and what Einstein called 'spooky action at a distance'. Mathematical constructions and proofs seem to have outrun practical hypotheses in this area. Maybe quantum mechanics is where classical physics was 100 years before Newton. Maybe we need a quantum Newton to help sort things out. Anyway, some people believe that electron entanglement, action at a distance and wave function collapse, may play a role in the complexity of image retrieval and therefore thinking, in human consciousness."

"Thanks Nigel. A short time ago, I asked Jonathan to summarize our discussion of this ultimate mystery of biology. To prepare, he has gone off to a favourite spot. I would ask you also to take the next few minutes to ponder consciousness before he returns. What a culmination that final understanding would be! Enough already, I'll be quiet."

Silence was wrapped in the sounds of summer and the sea.

"Here he comes," someone whispered.

Jonathan emerged from the trees, his lanky frame moving easily. The audience was unusually quiet as he mounted the tiny plateau, placed his notes on the lectern and stroked his beard. Just as he started to speak, a red squirrel chattered loud and long from a nearby tree, evoking laughter.

"He's voicing disapproval—the conscious little devil—even before I don't say nothin'," said Jonathan, recalling the plaintive complaint of a visiting five year old niece, "but I'll proceed. All right, we know the infrastructure of consciousness:

"Neural anatomy, fuels (glucose, oxygen), energy (electromagnetism), maintenance systems, (repair, defence, waste removal). The great puzzle is how the interaction of neural tissue and electromagnetism produces awareness. I suggest consciousness is a learned sensation aided and abetted by language acquisition.

"Think about it. The newborn has no sophisticated awareness, no memory of the first two years during which the nervous system is growing—prodded by incoming data. Consider two newborns: Baby A receives all the care and nurturing of adoring parents—even to hearing Mozart in the womb—taught continuously the names of sensations it receives, colours, numbers; language. Baby B is born in a cave, no light, sound, or any stimuli—an asensory environment. Compare the two in say six years; A will be brimming with—well—consciousness; awareness, emotions, thought; all the components of a thriving personality. B will, I think we can agree, and actually there have been cases recorded that mimic this situation, have minimal awareness, consciousness, and it will take years of sensory input for this child to become fully conscious. The anatomy, physiology, biochemistry were all the same. I therefore submit that our consciousness is a learned sensation.

"As a boy, I remember during a February nor'easter, leaving the light and warmth of our kitchen and walking into the cold, night-time scullery, which was filled with aromas of flour and corned beef. A window faced eastward into the black fury of a winter night. The house shook. I felt for the outdoor light switch. Suddenly, with a press of my finger, a wondrous scene was revealed; snowflakes—points of light—came swirling, dancing, floating more than anyone could imagine.

"Consciousness is like a blizzard, except every 'snowflake' is on a neurological path, has a sensory or motor role, is named and can be stored, retrieved, inhibited, or enhanced. And like snowflakes, can form drifts of thought, can wax into gusts of creativity, or wane into lulls of sleep. While the blizzard gets its energy from the wind, consciousness glows from the energy of the food we eat; both sources being the largest of our Mother sun. We, our bodies and our awareness, are stardust and star energy—an extension of the elegant physics of the universe."

In the silence that followed, Jonathan paused, picked up his papers and looked up at the black spruce. "See, our little furry friend is speechless!"

There was applause and laughter.

"Thanks so much Jonathan. Questions anyone?"

"What about soul, mind, spirit, subconscious, heart—do you reject all these?" asked Rachel, pushing her grey hair from her eyes.

"Good question, Mom," answered Jonathan, "actually all of these are synonyms attempting to label and explain the same thing; the extravagant blooming of our awareness. They imply connections beyond us with other imagined forces in the universe. But we have all these and more with our conscious awareness that reached its present profundity through gifts of stardust and energy from space. Surely we need nothing anymore romantic than this."

"What about the prevailing notion that religions are loving and moral while science is neither?"

"Another, with respect, very successful propaganda ploy. Science adds to the joy of existence; lowers the barriers of ignorance; fuels the creativity of unshackled intellect; and knowledge fathers morality. Just check out the truly secular democracies."

"So here, after all this fun and discussion is our considered definition of the big C: Human Consciousness is a product of the impact of electromagnetic energy on neurological tissue; the prolonged and varied repetition of which produces learned sensation that is abetted and sophisticated by language acquisition and growing memory resources."

The gang stood and applauded.

"Right on," said Matt. "It's almost time to party. Hey, Wilhelm, you've been quiet. It'll be your day tomorrow when we talk of human behaviour and whether man's intelligence can alter evolution."

Wilhelm looked gaunt and his smile was forced.

"I've enjoyed listening. Two days ago, I stood at the height of land on the Heart's Content barrens. Westward across the Bay, the blue hills of Trinity North were rumpled and ephemeral in sunshine interrupted by massive rainsqualls. It was a magnificent backdrop to wildflowers, barrens and wooded valleys that ran down to the sea. People here live in beautiful surroundings. They seem fascinated and entertained by the seasons and the cycles of species. They whirl, it seems, in a respectful but Darwinian dance, with the animate and inanimate of their island world. Their environment must mould behaviour.

"Someone mentioned the brain's anatomy and how parts persist there that reflect different stages of evolution—Primitive to Reptilian to Shakespeare. It mimics human behaviour. I look at that boat, that fisherman, peacefully employed, rounding the headland and think of what violence human beings, despite rationalism and a thick cerebral cortex, have committed ..." his voice broke. He stood up and walked down to the shore and stood looking out to sea. Vanessa walked over to comfort. She put an arm around his shoulder and they stood silhouetted against the light. The group was quietly restive.

"Well, that's it," said Matt. "We need some exercise, food and drink."

CHAPTER 48

▼

A crowd had gathered at the Shipman home, which stood 100 feet from the harbour shore. Sarah was a flurry of action in a kitchen full of grandchildren, sons, dogs, friends and just plain passersby, who had dropped in to find the source of aromas and the reason for an obvious increase in outport activity. Three fishermen, raw-boned and large, sat in one corner arguing, in accents loud, the politics of cod, their hands holding glasses filled with dark liquid.

"Cod out d'ere be da millions," said Simon Hiscock, his eyes, teeth and the beer-foam on his upper lip all a startling white against a red ochre face—the product of wind and sun on a reflecting sea. "Sure you can't get y'er line down 'cause dey'll pull it right out of y'er 'ands. 'Erbie Crocker, wit th' government license, caught a nation of fish in 'tree days."

"It's crazy," said Aaron Cumbie, smashing a huge fist down on the table, "dem fellers from th' government won't let a Newfoundlander catch a fish fer supper, while foreigners be's comin' into Placentia, unloading cod and halibut from th' Grand Banks and Newfound-landers buyin' it from dem! What a disgrace! I says if dem ol' fellers from years ago was back 'ere d'ered be war, yes b'y, war! But we 'aven't got it anymore. D'ere bribing' us wit' our own money."

The conference visitors all mixed in and the crowd flowed back and forth into the living and dining rooms. The stove was full of pots breathing steam and something fish-shaped hissed in a huge fry pan. The kitchen table was loaded with bread, vegetables, game, desserts and a large tub of lobsters.

"Come and help yarselves," yelled Sarah, in a voice that amazingly rose above the din. "Help yarselves and, if you don't, I could care less if y'se all bloody well starve!"

Wilhelm had slipped away into the front garden that sloped down to the sea, mysterious by moonlight. He had drunk the dark rum. He felt a strange mixture of euphoria and dread as the rum rattled his neurotransmitters. How had he played the game of life? They were singing inside. Maybe he could remember now and extirpate the ghosts. He looked seaward. He took a long drink. There was the face he remembered, the young giant who moved with ease and grace on the schooner, so powerful, so assured. Had he loved the young giant or was it hate? Now the fight, just a mile away, outside the harbour hills; gunshots, pain, the young man diving into the sea. Wilhelm remembered the twilight gleam on the gun barrel—the head in his sights; now gone, now there again, like a seal. He felt his finger pressure on the trigger, heard the explosion, saw the head fly apart and disappear—the water closing, leaving only a dark stain—dark like the water before him, like the rum in his glass.

Matt walked into the front garden with his dinner. He saw Wilhelm standing under the beech tree. The evening breeze stroked the sea and twilight was vermilion across the Bay.

Wilhelm embraced Matt and his face was strangely intent. His hair was white as foam and stood unruly at the sides like an egret in mating ritual. With a great effort he tried to break the strangle hold of memories. "This is all so lovely," he said. "All we need is Wagner, but that might be too much."

"Life is good," agreed Matt.

"Just look at that sea. I was thinking about the strange quandary of the human brain. This gem of biology, boxed in a rather tight bony cage, seems more concerned with the lifeless keratin that grows as hair on its outer layer than with itself. This brain seems to have the mother of all inferiority complexes, almost never tries to understand itself, and when it does, it ends up ascribing all its magnificent ability, all its potential reason, creativity and logic, to some outside mythical person or thing."

"Was it not Voltaire who said, 'a fanaticism composed of superstition and ignorance has been the sickness of all the centuries'?"

"Our brains, in an act of unspeakable obsequiousness, surrendered, spilled their magnificent potential upon desert sands to desiccate forever in the dry winds of mythology."

Tom arrived with a dark refill for the Captain.

"Anyway, I don't need to go on to you about these things. Let's celebrate the light of reason that appeared in the Orient, flashed in Greece and glows in European rationalism. Let's drink to the Gallileos, the Newtons, the Darwins and Einsteins who brought the light of knowledge to combat the ferocious behaviour of tribe, nation and race, caught in the thrall of superstition. May we finally rid ourselves of the colonialism of the God concept and treat our planet and ourselves with a rational respect."

"I'll drink to that."

Wilhelm raised his glass. "To you Matt and your friends—a Celtic toast:

> *May the deep peace of the running wave,*
> *The flowing wind,*
> *And the quiet earth,*
> *Be yours."*

The sounds of glasses clicking were lost to music from the house. A quartet had suddenly appeared. Tom played his guitar plus a mouth organ. A long-bearded man held an accordion. Someone pumped the ancient organ and a teenager stroked a mandolin. *'Me and Bobby McGee.' 'I'se the b'y.' 'Lights Along The Shore.'*

… Trim your feeble lamps my brothers,
Some poor sailor tempest tossed
Trying now to reach the harbour,
In the darkness may be lost …

By 1:00 a.m. the Shipman house was silent and the harbour quiet, except where the ocean pulse ebb-flowed wearily on its capillary shore, and an arrhythmic breeze sighed in the sleeping woods. A sly moon rose over the Mizzen hill. A rowboat floated near the shore, empty and free like a rider-less horse. Below the reflecting surface, a body lay in 12 feet of water—its elegant chemistry spent. The mouth was round as if howling and escaping air expanded upwards like bubbles in a glass of champagne. Wilhelm's corpse was twisted on itself and the right arm, tied to the anchor rode, floated up and waved slowly in the current. Beneath him, in the ribbed sea sand, snaked the copper sinews of the transatlantic cable.

Vanessa and Matt lay together in the cockpit of *Lorna Doone*. Surf sounded faintly from headlands darkened by moonlight.

"That was a great day," whispered Vanessa.

"Indeed it was. Let's hope we can get the celebrants together in the morning. There is much to elaborate and discuss."

"We still don't have a name for the book, but I have written a sample last paragraph."

"Really? Lets hear it," Matt said.

"It goes like this: Meanwhile we are alive, you and I. We have evolved down times 10 billion steps beneath our mother star. At our sensor tips we have the ferment of biology on planet Earth. We can view through slits in the electromagnetic spectrum the theatre of life and be part of the cast. We have everything in common with all living creatures and with the energy of the universe. Can we not love ourselves, each other and our friends of feather, fin and hoof? All life is stardust. We should celebrate."

"That's a prose poem and lovely," whispered Matt.

They embraced. The boat was quietly alive.

Later, Matt awakened. He saw Vanessa's face bathed in moonlight and the Red Ensign stirring on the taffrail. He thought of man—man who Alexander Pope had deemed 'The glory, jest and riddle of the world'. Here in this outport, lying tranquil and quiet in the moonlight, were all the sins and passions, all the felicity and kindness that raged elsewhere on the planet giving rise to terror and chaos, nobility and benevolence. Alexander Pope again, he thought.

> *Go wondrous creature mount where science guides,*
> *Go, measure earth, weigh air and state the tides;*
> *Instruct the planets in what orbs to run,*
> *Correct old time and regulate the sun …*
> *What reason weaves by passion is undone.*

"Maybe he should have used power rather than passion," thought Matt.

He stood up and moved carefully to the bow of *Lorna Doone*. Light reflected joyously off wavelets in the moon's wake. Phosphorescence clothed some creature that moved in the silent water. The sky was radiant with stars. He felt wonder and love, not just for this place, but for this earth, this precious home, floating in space tethered to the universe. This place where circumstance had conspired to produce combinations of its own substance that evolved to tears and joy. Whatever could heal the self-inflicted wounds of striving, anxious humanity?

Vanessa had written:

> *Has evolution erred*
> *And spawned a consciousness*
> *Susceptible to myth and cult'*
> *And all the blemishes that foul*
> *The lovely face of truth?*

"Mythology hasn't worked," he thought, "nor superstition. It's time indeed to rescue humanity from itself with the tonic of understanding and the morality of truth."

Epilogue

▼

Several years have passed. Many seasons have worked their magic on the Great Island; cycles of ice flows, caribou migrations, the ebb and flow of puffins and whales: the land changing robes from the russets of autumn to winter's shimmering white, the green of grudging spring and summer gold: a gentle people also on the move, from beloved outports to urban congregations and often to cities far away across the straits.

Vanessa and I live in a small house by the sea—actually the harbour. There is a garden out back and a city view in front, alive night and day and endlessly reflected in the water. There is also the glow of family and friends.

It may well be that, as we get older, our friends become dearer. One sees the tooth marks of time in faces and physiques and the realization dawns that we are all in a circle whose circumference is contracting toward a common center. The fires of youth burn down into a residue of doomed wisdom that has the poignancy of a brilliant autumn hillside awaiting the north wind. Together we form a mosaic of all that has gone before, the stamp of genetics, the recipe of chance, the relics of relationships and the responsibilities of reproduction. In essence, a similar experience to that of our forbearers stretching back into the mists of time.

After Prostner's suicide, we did not have a vacation-conference for two years; however, we kept in close contact via the marvellous new Internet, as science progressed dramatically, particularly in the areas of astrophysics and genetic engineering. Again, at the start of a century, a new theory sends a ripple of euphoria through the scientific community. The superstring theory, they say, has the potential to unite the physics of the very large with that of the very small, in one all encompassing theory of everything. Scientists throughout the planet strive to capture the theory in a mathematical net.

The idea is that quarks, electrons and all the fundamental particles consist of vibrating loops that can change shapes like the old Greek God, Proteus. These strings have resonant frequencies, like a violin. If a loop vibrates in one resonance it's an electron, another way it becomes a quark. My, oh my! The force particles, photons for example, are also string-loops and act the same way. They resonate and have harmonics. Indeed, the music of the spheres.

I was talking to my friend, Ernie, the other day and he says, "I like dem science fellers, but how can you take all this stuff serious, when they can't figure out if d'eres any cod in Trinity Bay?"

What an enigmatic life and ironic death was Prostner's! There is a police photo of the body under water and you would swear it was giving the Nazi salute. He never escaped being caught in the monstrous events of the 1940's and nobody, probably not even himself, could decide what his role had been. The dramatic and tragic events involving U694 and the schooner *Blackduck* off Heart's Content split public opinion almost evenly as to whether Prostner was a villain or a British spy. The media never tired of him. There was talk of a movie. Prostner's writings reveal an obsession to discover what underlies man's penchant to follow leaders blindly—both real and mythical—and to commit the most grotesque crimes while in that thrall. Here is an excerpt from one of his essays:

'Nietzsche made the necessary intellectual progress in his youth to discard religion. He early stood with his intellect unfettered—a brilliant mind with unlimited potential.

He, however, failed. He mistook the eradication of religion as producing a void rather than as removing an obstacle. He substituted a lunatic's society destined only for abuse and anarchy. With religion removed, the road is cleared for humanity, grouped as democracies, where the individual has unlimited potential to savour the reality of his situation through the collective reasoning of humankind.

The greatest pleasure is the contemplation of nature and the understanding of how the universe and biology came about. This leads to an enhanced evaluation of self and increased respect for all creatures.

It also imposes a calm, a quiet ecstasy, as opposed to the anxious tyrannical group of insanities and subservience imposed by power-abusing myth—dynasties.'

We had fun picking a name for the book. Jonathan wanted, 'This Above All', but I recalled a book by that name that had thrilled me in my youth: a story about a spitfire pilot and his English amour having an affair on the white cliffs with buzz bombs overhead. Hemmingway gets the nod for titles. He literally took names from the Bible and John Donne—*The Sun also Rises* and *For Whom the Bell Tolls*. We found some marvellous lines in Omar Khayyam and Gray's Elegy, but none short enough. Vanessa likes Stardust, but Jonathan and I think 'The Dawning' indicates what we are trying to get across.

Some of the old crowd is gone. Both Tom and Sarah are in the cemetery that overlooks the Mizzen pond. At the last, Tom, eyes closed, recognized my handclasp.

"That's Doc, isn't it?" he whispered, then with a trace of a smile, "Sure, doc is only cod spelled backwards," and he died.

Nigel is still alive—very much so. He married a Belgian princess when he was 72 and they are busy restoring a castle which he purchased in Wales. He still has *Lorna Doone*.

Rachel's life turned out to be a flourish—a pirouette in the face of fortune. Her late career in telemedicine as a member of the Dr. Rouse team, which achieved international attention, made her a household name on the Island and Labrador. On one occasion, under UN auspices, she visited the University of Maiduguri in northern Nigeria. It was during the military dictatorship. She was caught up in religious strife and held hostage for nine days by the Muslims before her release was brokered. She was in poor shape mainly because of an attack of malaria. After she retired, she lived quietly in Heart's Content until she joined Sam and some of Wilhelm's ashes overlooking the Clam Brook.

Professor Moore died just 3 months ago. He was biking with a new girlfriend on the Appalachian Trail. We don't know the exact circumstances. His age had to be close to 3 digits. For years. he wrote a science column for a major New York newspaper.

Here is an example:

'Biology can be regarded as a great sphere expanding continuously from the moment of the Big Bang—or the first replicating molecule, if you wish—until now. The circumference of this huge ball is always at the tip of the arrow of time; it is where we are at this and every instant. This sphere, which began with biology's infinite potential, now has a pocked surface and an interior like Swiss cheese, representing millions, aye, billions, of species that have lived and left hollow branches of extinction in Darwinian death. The remaining structure consists of present day species in dynamic evolution.'

As a poet friend put it:

> *Biology grows in spherical array,*
> *Child of the quantum burst,*
> *That set the stage on which strode C and H and O,*
> *Electrified!*
> *Particles invisible entwined*

Spawned symmetries
That anticipate the mammal's eye
Projection on cerebral screens,
And consciousness.

Jonathan and family are well. He is more relaxed now that the hydro problem with Quebec is finally resolved. Too bad the solution had to be so drastic, but at least we've regained a little dignity. He wrote a book called, '*From DNA to the Internet*'. It attributes the ascent of Homo sapiens to four giant steps: DNA and its protein wealth of reproducible design; the evolutionary leap forward of the cerebral cortex with its prodigious capacity for data reception and memory; the creation of schools and libraries that prevented generational loss of learning, and the Internet as a massive extension of the cerebral cortices and libraries.

"Hey, Vanessa, there's Richard Tauber singing '*Vienna My City of Dreams*'. Turn it up please! Listen … Music, ah music! As Keats wrote: '*Music's golden tongue flattered to tears, this aged man*'. How wonderful it is!"

This morning we watched dawn illuminate the city. Light came like a concept through the Narrows, its artistry enhanced by the clarity of the air. The dark houses put on Joseph's coat. Ships and spires emerged from the trance of night, trees and flowers dressed splendidly for the day. Was it not light like this that long ago washed Athena's temple on a Grecian hill?

Now it is afternoon and time for Vanessa and me to take a walk through the village below the cliffs. Just a few hundred yards farther along the coastal trail, you can listen by a huge cleft in the rock and hear the ocean's rhythmic seethe in dark caverns. We will sit on blackberry moss, among wild roses, and smell the headlands. Maybe we will see a whale, or an iceberg. Certainly, there will be ships. Then we will walk home and have tea.

Here, from perspectives new
We sense ancestral lives
That heard time's music on these moody shores
And here high on a seaward peak
In friendship's thrall
We share a painted moment
And are gone

978-0-595-46049-6
0-595-46049-6

LaVergne, TN USA
22 August 2010
194097LV00003B/6/P